Winslow
in Love

Also by Kevin Canty

A Stranger in This World
Into the Great Wide Open
Nine Below Zero
Honeymoon and Other Stories

Nan A. Talese

Doubleday

New York

London   Toronto   Sydney   Auckland

Winslow in Love

Kevin Canty

PUBLISHED BY NAN A. TALESE

AN IMPRINT OF DOUBLEDAY

a division of Random House, Inc.

1745 Broadway, New York, New York 10019

DOUBLEDAY is a registered trademark of Random House, Inc.

This book is a work of fiction. Names, characters, businesses, organizations, places, events, and incidents either are the product of the author's imagination or are used fictitiously. Any resemblance to actual persons, living or dead, events, or locales is entirely coincidental.

Book design by Terry Karydes

Library of Congress Cataloging-in-Publication Data

Canty, Kevin.

Winslow in love / Kevin Canty.—1st ed.

p.   cm.

1. College teachers—Fiction. 2. Separated people—Fiction. 3. Alcoholics—Fiction. 4. Montana—Fiction. 5. Poets—Fiction. I. Title.

PS3553.A56W56 2004

813'.54—dc22

2004051754

ISBN 0-385-51366-6

PRINTED IN THE UNITED STATES OF AMERICA

March 2005

FIRST EDITION

1   3   5   7   9   10   8   6   4   2

for Denise Shannon

Winslow
in Love

The rain fell on downtown Portland, not in any kind of unusual way. It was four-thirty on a December afternoon and Winslow, drunk, sat by the front window of Kelly's Olympian and watched the passersby. The afternoon was fading fast and the faces were darkening outside, unfurling their umbrellas against the rain, hurrying toward their buses and cars and taxicabs and appointments, everybody rushing toward their own deaths, Winslow thought, and none of them knew it.

He had a pack of Tareytons and a pitcher of draft beer and the daily papers, the *Oregonian* and the *New York Times* both. He read the local paper carefully from back to front, from sports to news, and then went back through the *Times* to see what he had missed. When an item struck his imagination he would sometimes write a sentence or two down in his notebook. He kept the notebook in his overcoat pocket, as he was not the type to write ostentatiously in bars or coffee shops. Just then he felt an image coming up to the surface, something about the faces outside the window, like a whole school of fish turning at once, the silvery bodies in three dimensions, something about the way they didn't recognize themselves as beautiful but just kept on schooling to their separate ends. Then remembered that Pound had gotten there first: *petals on a wet, black bough* . . . It was not fair that so many of his best ideas were someone else's.

The bar was long and dim with neon lights high up against an old tin ceiling. A kitchen at the far back contributed the smell of stale fryer oil to the general funk of spilled beer, cigarette smoke and Lysol. Toothlessness and vomit; he watched a pair of old girls going at it, shoving each other against the bar, cursing. One of them he recognized as the folding-chair woman, a tiny short angry woman who had been beating the day bartender with a metal folding chair the first day he had found Kelly's. The bartender was at least eighteen inches taller than she was and had an earring and his head shaved like Mr. Clean. He stood impassively with his arms folded in front of him while she beat against him with the folding chair until she wore herself out, and then he 86'd her. She had been 86'd by every bartender so far, but the turnover was high on the day shift and so she was back.

Later, when the light outside died completely, Winslow would move back to sit at the bar, where generations of drinkers had worn grooves into the top by rubbing quarters back and forth on the wood, the knurled metal edges digging deep smooth trenches into the bar, and nobody minded.

In the last months, he had seen youth in the bar, the black t-shirt and black leather crowd, and soon it would be over and the last downtown bar would be gone and Portland would have finished turning into something else and it would be time to move on. Not yet.

So much money in town now, he thought. So much success. A little failure kept him honest.

Winslow stubbed his cigarette out and laid the butt in the ashtray in a parallel line with the rest of the afternoon's dead soldiers. They were each smoked down to half an inch from the filter, each the same length, each lined up neatly with the others. The rain was coming down a little harder now, the pedestrians all walking faster or sleek under dark umbrellas and dark overcoats but still hurrying before their shoes got wet, all hurrying toward drinks or dates or a last appointment, all holding the city in the air between them, Winslow thought, a city made not from bricks and concrete and asphalt but by the intentions and desires of the souls who lived in it. Everybody wanted something. Everybody wanted the same thing, lately: money, success, a mistake-free life, a life without enemies. All these intersecting desires, colluding, colliding, all this assorted *valence*, with some of them missing an electron in the outer shell and some of them with an extra electron . . . Wisdom from the Army: he remembered Solomon Jackson, the look in his red, diseased eyes when he said: You want to live without enemies. You're afraid to make enemies.

Later on they became friends. After that, Solomon died. Winslow slumped back against the well-worn wooden bench, his hands splayed out in front of him, like a priest's hands, open and fat. The light was delicate and gray. Winslow himself was fat and bald and drunk but at least he was clean, he was scrupulous about that. He wore a white shirt and a tweed sport jacket. He sat back waiting for whatever the afternoon would bring him, and after that the evening.

He was watching the sky when June Leaf came in. He didn't see her until she sat down across from him and poured her own clean glass full from what was left of Winslow's beer.

"You fucker," she said. "I thought you were working."

"I was," he said.

He pushed the pack of cigarettes over to her but she shook her head. June Leaf smoked three a day but this wasn't the time.

"What happened?" she said.

"I came to a spot," he said. "It just seemed like a moment to take a break."

"How long have you been here?"

He held the pitcher at an angle so the beer ran down into a corner of it. "Just this," he said.

"Don't you lie to me."

Winslow looked at her: something in her voice, some new aggravation. It was a small lie, one pitcher short of the truth, and, besides, June Leaf was not an innocent herself. She drank the first glass of beer in a hurry and then poured herself another out of the rest of Winslow's beer, leaving him half a glass away from dry. Then she shook the cigarette out of the pack and looked around to see who she knew. Eddie in the plastic pants waved back at her. She regarded Winslow through the haze of her smoke.

"Did you get anything done today?" she asked.

"Enough," he said. "I paid my debt to society."

She knew he was not telling the truth—Winslow could feel it, the way her eyes glanced off his face—but she didn't take him up on it. This was marriage in Winslow's experience: knowing the other well enough to know she was lying but not well enough to know why. June Leaf settled into the opposite chair, a tall thin angular woman all in black, half a head taller than Winslow, people stared when they went out. She craned around to watch the dim afternoon outside.

"Nice light," she said. "Filthy weather, though. You got a call this afternoon."

Winslow waited for the rest of it, watching her hands in the soft enveloping light, as she was watching her hands herself. She stubbed out her cigarette haphazardly in the ashtray, ruining his careful alcoholic symmetry. June Leaf was a painter, though lately she had been supporting both of them as a claims adjuster for Kaiser. Winslow was fifty-five and she was forty-one and they had been married three years. They met in Mexico.

"Who did I get a call from?" he finally asked.

"It was Jack Walrath, over in Athens?" June Leaf said. Winslow felt his heart race inside him, this new call to glory, a voyage to Greece; and June Leaf must have seen it on his face as she quickly added, "Not *that* Athens. The one in Montana."

Winslow remembered Walrath then, a fool, a fixer, a second-rate poet. "What did he want?"

She said, "Apparently a visiting writer canceled out on them and now they want you."

"For what?"

"A semester, is what he said. Twenty-five thousand dollars and an apartment, is what he said."

"Oh, shit," Winslow said.

He looked at her face in the fine soft light of the window, long and lined, dark eyes, dark lips, the beautiful hollow at the base of her throat. She looked tired, he thought.

"What's wrong?" she said. "I thought you'd be happy about it."

Winslow hadn't written anything worth reading for eighteen months. He knew that for a fact, knew that as well as he knew his own name, and the thought of trying to tell anyone anything about poetry made him ill. The idea of standing up in a classroom again, which he had done before, and pretending that he knew anything about it. He should have told her before, should have confirmed what June Leaf suspected: that he spent his working hours in idleness and masturbation. The enterprise of poetry had defeated him entirely.

He should have told her but he had not, and now it was too late. June Leaf had been supporting both of them, with small exceptions. It came down to the money.

June Leaf looked at him warily. "I thought you'd be happy about it," she said again.

"No, it's good," he said. "It's a good thing."

She knew him well enough to disbelieve him.

"Well, I'm celebrating," she said, taking the empty beer pitcher from the table. "I'm drinking gin myself. Do you want anything? Or are you going to keep on drinking beer?"

"Scotch on the rocks," he said automatically, watching her skinny ass recede into the gathering crowd around the bar. It would take her a few minutes to get the bartender's attention, which was good. Winslow would try to compose himself, try to be happy, as she believed he should be. To feel the proper emotions. What one ought to feel.

She had told him before—she was feeling it now—that she felt invisible sometimes, that Winslow was the only living being in Winslow's world, that everybody else including her was just furniture. He didn't know that she was wrong. He hoped she was wrong but he didn't know. Did he love her? Winslow didn't know. He felt some deep stirring inside him but whether it was what other people called love or not was a mystery.

But *solvent*, Winslow thought. Money in the bank, money in his pocket. Back to being the overdog. He knew it wasn't good for him but still.

Somewhere outside, past the edge of the city and even in the city itself, in the dark dripping passages between buildings and the blackberry brambles along the edges of the railroad cuts, water was dripping over dark leaves, animals were moving through the undergrowth, the steelhead were making their way up-stream from the Pacific. *Anadromous*, he thought. Oregon out there in the rain.

"What's the matter with you?" June Leaf said. She set the bar glass down on the table in front of him and Winslow saw that it was a double: happy hour.

"The long illness of my life," he said, and both of them laughed and drank. "When does all this start?" he asked. "When does he want me over there?"

"The semester starts the end of January."

"Dear God," said Winslow. "We're moving to the North Pole."

"*You're* moving," June Leaf said.

Later: fat man in the bathtub. This was where he did his thinking, after a fashion, whatever you called it when the brain was trying to surface through a sheen of alcohol. June Leaf was at her studio painting, or whatever she did when she was there, she erased—it seemed like—more than she ever painted. And everything was fine with her after the evening. There were cocktails, which made everything fine.

Winslow floated. There was enough of him to make it perilous to move, there was sloshing and splashing and water spilled on the tile floor of June Leaf's apartment. Though he lived there now, too, though they were as married as they were ever going to get, it was still and would be forever June Leaf's apartment. Until the landlord got them out. Floor by floor, apartment by apartment, the old tenants were leaving and the landlord was remodeling in their wake. The flat below, where Mrs. Esterhazy had said her last words in Hungarian—said them to Winslow, who had found her with a broken hip on the stairs and carried her inside—was now the nest of a pair of cuckoobirds with square granny glasses and the girl had pink hair. Everything was broken.

Winslow watched his dick float limp in the water, his gray seaweed.

Winslow tried to think of what he could tell the children of Athens about poetry. He had not started out feeling like a Latin teacher but by now he did, the lame protest that poetry was good for you, that poetry built intellect and character, that captains of industry and powerful men had all grown up on poetry, stupid enough even if it was not a lie, which it was. The captains of industry had grown up on touch football and beer. They liked red meat and heterosexual sex. Even Mrs. Esterhazy, who could have used a little, had lived and died entirely without poetry. The men at the paper mill where his father had worked, the television-loving millions, they were better off without it. Selling little ego pills: *You* can make this work, little Susie, little Ned. *You* can make this somehow matter, though the rest of us have failed.

He would teach them Rilke. They would like Rilke—the sponger, the rich woman's amusement with his angels and vapors. It would serve them right. They would leave him alone. If they didn't like it, he would make them all read Gertrude Stein and then pretend to understand it. What do you mean, little Susie, little Ned, that you don't *get it*? Why are you so worried about *getting it*?

Something about the prospect of teaching brought out the sadist in him. But Winslow felt better now. He had a game plan. He nudged the hot-water tap open with his foot and felt the healing waters spill over him, took a sip from the icy glass of scotch on the edge of the tub and settled back again, listening to Ellington in the next room. The bathroom ceiling was almost ten feet high so the heights of the room almost disappeared in the steam, a yellowing waterspotted dimness in the incandescent light, a color out of favor now. Everything was white or blue-white now, all cool and clean. No more octagonal tile, no more wainscoting, no more faintly dirty butter-colored light. *We are the bees of the invisible,* Rilke said. At times Winslow could almost make sense of it. He lit a cigarette and lay back in the water.

Then it was four in the morning and he was awake. He had slept, what? from nine or ten till four. This was not the morning after he found out but another morning, or another. Any morning you could find him, although the clock mysteriously turned off on weekends and let him sleep till seven or eight. Any morning you would see him slip out of bed, clean from his bath the night before, naked and nimble. He loved to sleep naked, loved to feel the boy's body encased somewhere in the layers of fat but released in sleep. You would see him slip out of the bedroom and make his coffee and sit, industrious, at his dining-room table with a pencil and a pad of white paper and wait.

Or else he would slip on his eyeglasses, which made him look owlish and professorial, and maintain his correspondence on an old Olivetti portable typewriter, which he appeared to be trying to wrestle to the table. June Leaf, a night owl, slept with eyeshades and earplugs. The gooneybirds downstairs complained that they could hear the pounding of the keys through the legs of the table and through the floor and their ceiling, and Winslow believed them.

Or else he would go to the window and watch the slow dawn creep over Northwest Portland, the shine of wet asphalt under an asphalt-colored sky.

Or else he would read: anything, he would read anything, he opened and read the fake U.S.-government envelopes that the mortgage company sent to June Leaf. Winslow was the last man in America who didn't have a credit card. He read Auden sometimes to make himself feel worse. Or else he would examine *The Tempest* in the company of Auden, he would keep company with Caliban and Ariel for a while and talk to Auden, agreeing and disagreeing with him as he read, until Winslow felt so exalted, so honored to be part of this endless ongoing conversation about what was true and what was beautiful and what was good, that when it ended, when he found himself at the table again with his blank legal pad again and nothing to say and nothing to show for it, Winslow just wanted a drink, and sometimes he had one. Six-thirty in the morning. Quarter to eight.

This was where his Lincoln Town Car came from: five years before (it seemed like another life, a page from somebody else's biography) Winslow had gotten interested in narration.

It occurred to him at the time that he had been living his entire life in a lyrical mode; that he had been seeing his life and the world around him as a series of bright moments, connected by passages of time in which nothing much of interest happened, getting in and out of cars, shopping for groceries, attending to the post office and so on. He was still working for the hospital at the time as he had for twenty years, writing press releases and internal newsletters, wearing his suits from Penney's and his polyester-blend shirts (which he still wore). It was easy to imagine those hours as nothing more than passage-work, the things between the important things, which struck Winslow as no way to live.

At some point Winslow decided that he was tired of the lyrical mode and decided to give narration a try: an accumulating series of events, like a nice solid house, brick by brick.

He settled on a story from his own high-school days about a girl that Winslow himself had not gone out with. She lived in Mist, an actual town not far from Jewell, where Winslow had grown up. She lived and waited with her mother on the edge of town in a trailer that was slowly melting into the landscape, the Oregon rain and Oregon greenery, the tin of the trailer itself slowly turning green with mold and rot and the ferns growing up around it. Her father had gone missing in Korea and everybody knew he was dead. But her mother had seen his face—it had to be his face—in the background of a newsreel once and had fainted in the Seaside theater where she saw it and then had called her congressman and sued the newsreel company and spent all the insurance money to go to Japan, where she couldn't get a passport for Korea.

In life the daughter was a plain-faced girl who liked sports and later went on to become an assistant district attorney in Seattle. She went out one summer with a friend of Winslow's and she actually fucked him, which was unique. Winslow's friend, a boy named Dougie, described the experience in detail, such specific detail that it sent Winslow into a fit of longing from which it seemed like he had never recovered: it happened in a pup tent by a lake in the Cascades, on an outing sponsored by her church group.

In the long narrative poem that Winslow wrote about her, nothing of the plain-faced girl survived. She became willowy and wan, the lake water on her bare breasts sparkled in the sunlight, etc. In a certain light, you could argue that the whole thing was a sentimental piece of shit. She died, in the poem, and the central character—named, of course, "I"—learned and grew. In other moments Winslow thought he recognized himself, a little of himself in the suffering narrator, a little survival of that old longing somehow fixed upon the surface of the page. Which was all he asked for, all he ever asked for: a little something on the page.

Also, the plain-faced girl herself—by now a plain-faced woman—came to a reading he gave in Seattle and said, "That's me, isn't it? That's me in your book."

Winslow told her that it was and she kissed him, right there in the bookstore.

"I knew it was," she said. "I read about it in the paper and as soon as I saw your name I knew it. All that business with my mother. That girl is having so much more fun than I ever did, that girl in your book. I'm jealous."

So much more fun than I ever did . . . When Winslow thought back to that book—which was nearly popular, a book which people read, and wrote him letters about—the only thing he had gotten out of it was a kiss, the plain-faced woman's kiss. It was worth having written the book just to see her, just to see how pleased she was to find herself in that light in it. That's me, he thought. That's me. If only she had kissed him like that *once* in high school, if only anybody had, his life would have been completely different. Winslow was sure of it.

Also, he got a Lincoln Town Car out of the deal. A minor star, a girl in Hollywood who was trying to improve herself, stumbled onto his book and fell in love. Her name was "attached" to the book; she was famous enough so that two different producers each took out options on his poem, at fifty thousand dollars a pop, but not so famous that anybody would actually make a movie out of it.

Winslow withstood the first fifty thousand but when the second fifty thousand came, a year later, he broke under the pressure. He quit his job at the hospital and bought the Lincoln. He could feel his luck changing. The curve was good. Not only was he going to be the most famous poet in America, he was going to be popular among the youth, every minor star would clamor for his next book. None of this made sense—he knew better, even while it was happening—but it all had a certain logic that he couldn't seem to stop. How, after all, could Winslow be expected to revolutionize American literature while holding down a nine-to-fiver at St. Patrick's? The place on Olympus was his for the taking if only he had the nerve. Risks, yes, there were risks. But greatness does not stop for danger.

He still had the car at least. The house and that particular marriage had fallen away but he still had the car; eleven years old now and a hundred and ten thousand miles on it but it still purred like a kitten going down the road and the seats were leather and wide as any Barcalounger. This was a car that had not lost its nerve: wide, long, powerful, invisible—so far—to police. Let the little people drive Toyotas. It had a powerful radio, too, that seemed to be able to pick up stations from far away, especially at night. Winslow loved few things more than driving at night, sipping beer under the stars and listening to Toronto, Albuquerque, San Diego, the weather in Houston or a ball game out of St. Louis.

That night in January he was pulling a steady seventy under a full moon between Kennewick and Ritzville, the atomic scablands of eastern Washington. June Leaf sat inscrutable in the seat beside him and Stan Kenton was coming in from a radio station far away, fading in and out as the hills rolled under his wheels. But still, Winslow thought: Stan Kenton. It felt like a blessing.

Outside the windshield was dark and cold with a little powdery snow blowing across the headlights. The motel—they had a reservation in Spokane—was still two hours away.

"Are we there yet?" June Leaf said.

"We are," said Winslow. "We are exactly here."

"Is there anything to drink?"

"Open the glovebox."

June Leaf did, and there in the glove compartment light was a flat brown pint of Johnnie Walker. She opened it—the crack of plastic separating from plastic—and took a drink; handed it to Winslow and he drank, resealed it, put it back, shut the lid.

"What happens if you get pulled over?" she asked.

"I keep the registration here," he said, pulling the sun visor down, showing her the little flap on the back where the insurance card and registration lay folded.

"Thank you so much," said June Leaf.

"What?"

"I've been driving around for three years and not knowing there was a bottle in there," she said. "What if I got pulled over?"

"You never did," he said. "Besides, you don't drive this car much."

"Enough," she said.

"It's usually under the seat anyway," he said. "What are we fighting about?"

"Nothing," she said.

"It's just a few months," he said.

"I don't know why you're trying to talk me into it," June Leaf said. "I was the one who had to talk *you* into it when this whole thing started. It's a fine idea. I can be there this week and then you can come over to Portland for the break in March."

"No, that's right."

The road came toward them now in flurries of snow that broke through the headlights and over the glass, inches in front of their faces. It seemed to Winslow that he hadn't seen another car in a while.

"Besides, it doesn't matter," June Leaf said. "We need the money."

"Well, that's right," Winslow said.

"I didn't say anything."

"You didn't have to."

"I can't stand this, Richard. First I have to pay the rent and then I have to feel shitty about it afterward."

She took the Johnnie Walker out of the glovebox again and took a long pull off the bottle. Then put it back again without offering it to Winslow.

"Hey," he said.

"You're driving."

"So what?"

"It's snowing, Richard."

Winslow reached over and opened the glovebox again himself and took the pint out and sipped from it, no more than a sip. But he closed the glovebox door again and left the bottle on the armrest between them. Stan Kenton faded out on the radio, replaced by a rush of silvery static that sounded to Winslow exactly how the snow looked coming through the headlights: between stations, nothing, nowhere.

"We should go back," he said.

"We can't go back."

"We can go anyplace we want to," Winslow said. "It wouldn't be the first time a poet didn't show up someplace. It's an occupational hazard. Look at this."

He waved his hand at the snow outside.

"It's just suffering," he said. "How much suffering do you need?"

This time it was June Leaf's turn to take a swallow from the bottle. Winslow was tempted to follow her but he was driving, she was right, miles to go before Spokane and no sign of the snow abating. A surge of belief welled up inside him: Winslow was right! They had no business in Montana, it was only suffering waiting for them there.

"Let's go to California," he said. "Someplace where the sun shines. Let's go to Berkeley. I could find a job in Berkeley."

"You'd die in California," June Leaf said. "You need the rain. All that sunny weather, you'd just shrivel up like a bug."

"I could be happy," Winslow said. "I could try."

"You wouldn't last ten minutes."

"I could be miserable in a place where it doesn't snow," he said. "I had forgotten about the snow."

"I don't think California," June Leaf said.

"Then home."

June Leaf didn't say anything. Winslow shook a Tareyton out of the pack on the dash and found his lighter in his shirt pocket, everything where it ought to be here in the space station, hurtling forward through the dark. He lit the cigarette and in the light of the flame he saw June Leaf's face reflected in the glass of the windshield and she looked gaunt and tragic. It was terrible, the way she looked. Her face remained imprinted on him after the flame was gone. It took him a moment to work up the nerve to ask.

"What's the matter?"

"Nothing," she said. "Let's just have a good time this week."

Nothing more was said but Winslow understood. It was interesting the way good news could suddenly change into bad news without anything being any different. He felt quite suddenly free and light, as if the movement of the car would carry him free of the earth in a moment, around the next curve, at the crest of the next hill—unencumbered and light and ready to fly. This was the wrong thing to feel, he knew it. June Leaf was leaving, for a while, for good, she didn't know herself. And Winslow loved her. He wasn't done with her, as she appeared to be with him.

But Winslow also trusted her, and knew that she was smarter than he was when it came to these matters. He never knew what was happening while it was happening to him, never understood until some years had gone by and he tried to write about it. June Leaf was leaving, he heard her say so, unless he was mistaken. Was this good? Was this necessary? He wouldn't know. Winslow felt his own sadness from a great height looking down, like a character in a play, sorrow and pity mixed.

But also this lightness. This joy. What had turned him around so? He couldn't even feel what he was supposed to feel.

"I've only ever been here once before," June Leaf said. "Did I tell you this?"

"No," he said. "I don't think so."

"I was in college, I think. Maybe the summer between high school and college. I came out west—I'd never been out west before—some job my mother found me at this place called Swanson's Mountain View Lodge. It was beautiful—beautiful in this kind of simple way, you know? I didn't like it at first. After a while, though . . ."

She went on with her story, and on, and Winslow relaxed into his leather throne, piloting the giant car through the snow, taking occasional light sips of scotch and feeling the rush of movement, the comfort of her company, the illusion—already going away, already fleeting, and all the better for it—of his own happiness. Something would happen next. Something always did. But he was all right for now, all right for now, the rhythm of the tires of the big Lincoln roaring forward through the snow and the comfort of her voice, her story. All right for now.

But in the first light of morning, waking up in the Ramada on the outskirts of Spokane, he remembered: *Let's just have a good time this week.*

Outside the window in the parking lot clean white people in ski clothes were loading up their Suburbans for a day on the slopes. Gray skies, a powdery dusting of new snow and the old snow wadded up in the corners of the parking lot. The Rocky Mountains loomed in the distance, over a middle distance of industrial afterthoughts and gray suburbs. June Leaf lay sprawled on the bed in the posture of a dead person, half snoring. She slept like she'd been shot.

Winslow had been awake for an hour or more in the dark. Once he was awake there was no going back, but these mornings, with no privacy and nowhere to write, were hell itself. Not that the writing was any better, not lately, but the nothing was worse. The habit had been a part of him for so long: The early mornings, everybody asleep but Winslow, the way the day would center itself around the blank piece of paper. Waiting to see what would happen, how he would fill it up. And even if the words had stopped coming, there was always the waiting. The thing he was: waiting.

He lay and listened to June Leaf breathe—the heavy, half-dead breathing of the drunk—and thought about all he had had to drink the night before: the rest of the pint from the car, then several cans of beer and the other pint, which had been in the trunk. A moment of panic when he remembered that they had finished it and it was Sunday morning but then he remembered they were going into Montana, where you could buy on Sundays. That made how many drinks? *Enough* by any means of keeping score. Counting up, Winslow felt the old dread creeping over him, the certainty that there was something wrong with him, something poisoned and incurable. This was how his father went, the little house in Jewell with the satellite dish outside and the cheap wine.

But this was a matter he had already decided. Winslow was not going to get better. He had resolved in fact to stop feeling guilty. He was who he was, he was born broken. It would make as much sense to feel guilty about his baldness, which in fact he did. At this hour of the morning he could feel that anything was his fault: the fat, the drinking, the gray light of morning creeping across Spokane.

Clean, clean, always clean. He showered without waking June Leaf and pulled on chinos and a white dress shirt and descended into the lobby in search of coffee. The daylit man, clean and sensible.

Several families of the ski people were in the lobby enjoying the complimentary continental breakfast, which to Winslow meant a breakfast with a spare-tire carrier in the middle of the trunk lid, but never mind. His own Lincoln wasn't continental anywhere, not anymore. As usual Winslow had missed it. He poured a cup of weakling coffee and selected a pair of Danishes—cream cheese, raspberry—from the Plexiglas dome. The television was blaring overhead, the morning news, some new disaster and Americans dead, and there was no place to sit outside the dangerous radiation of the television light, no place for Winslow. America was having breakfast with the TV on. America had rejected Winslow outright, chewed him up and spit him back out.

In flight from the television racket Winslow took his pastries down the hall and into the indoor pool. Here he was alone; or so he thought at first. The daylight thinned to a watery blue through the condensation on the windows, and the slap and tickle of the water against itself echoed off the tiles and made a nice indeterminate racket. He settled himself into a tropical chair of white metal and plastic strapping and thought of the snow blowing around in the parking lot, the gray skies outside; even the light was more cheerful here, though the smell of chlorine in the air was nearly intolerable, acrid and sharp. One of those smells, though, like two-stroke motor oil or suntan lotion, which were inextricably bound up with the ideas of summer and youth and health.

Who? he said experimentally, just to listen to the echo, and the sound came back to him from all directions and lingered: Ooooooh . . .

A body disengaged itself from the spa at the far end of the room, where she had been lying quietly and alone. Tall and naked—or so it seemed to Winslow; his glasses had fogged up when he came into the pool room and he had wiped them inadequately on the hem of his shirt—she stood indifferently and wrapped her hair in a towel and then pulled on a white bathrobe and left by the far door.

Winslow wiped his glasses again but by then she was gone, if she had ever been there—it was unclear, what he had seen, what had announced itself to him. Then felt her, the disappearing woman, felt her naked body inside him. Where was that part of him? That missing bravado and daring? You did it, whatever it was. You did it and then apologized later, if you still felt like apologizing, which Winslow never did. It was Winslow's fault. Winslow had interrupted her naked morning. She was unashamed and angry at him for disturbing her. I need that, Winslow thought: that daring, whatever it was called. That sense that the world belonged to him. Everything good that had ever happened to Winslow had come out of that feeling and now it was gone from him.

He understood now about June Leaf.

He understood that June Leaf wanted to be paid back. Not necessarily in money—though he understood how wearing it could be, having to do all the thinking about money, all the doing about money—but paid back in some species of currency, in poetry or money or sex or fun. Winslow had none of these things. He was tapped out.

It was not about love or the absence of love. He had let the account get too far out of balance, that was all. In some way this was hopeful: if he could right himself, if he could bring something to her, he could even things out again and they could start again. This was not out of the picture. He sipped his coffee, contemplating how this might happen. But all he found in his store of ideas were the old dreams of glory, the Notional Book Award and the Foolitzer Prize, girl-poets strewing rose petals as they carried him through the streets. . . . It was terrible how much he wanted, how immodest and immoderate he was in his dreams and how little he settled for. Not a word worth reading in two years now and still he had his ambitions.

He would go to Athens and he would take his medicine. Then they would see.

He finished his coffee in the chair by the pool and waited for some new idea to come to him. Still undermined by the presence of that naked body, half seen, all the things he wasn't, he felt the throb of spent alcohol running through him. He felt the next thing coming, although he didn't know what it would be. First there had to come the crash, then the recovery. That was what the naked woman was telling him: First there had to come the crash. Then the next thing could come.

He finished his coffee and Danishes and went back into America for more, carrying—a walking comedy routine—a Sunday paper and two coffees and pastries for June Leaf down the long hospital-smelling corridor, the doors all alike, the different lives behind each one. The wrong card, the wrong key, the wrong door. Just walk in and take your place in somebody else's life. It could happen.

He fumbled his way into the room, although not without having to set the paper cups of coffee down on the carpet. June Leaf was in the shower when he came in and Winslow felt like he was already invited, like the naked woman had already invited him. He set the American breakfast down on the plastic table and shed his clothes and felt the damp, sterilized air circulate around his nakedness. She was neither surprised nor unsurprised when he let himself into the steamy glass booth but turned away from him wordlessly. The shower booth stood alone along one wall of the bathroom like the secret booth they used to have on quiz shows, a place for the contestant to be alone while everybody else learned the answers. Just knowing this made Winslow feel like the oldest man in the world. He soaped her back: the long bamboo cane of her spine. She turned and took him in her hand and then, two slippery fish, inside. With his eyes closed they were young and strong and beautiful.

Afterward he sat with a towel around his waist feeling kingly with the heat turned all the way up. June Leaf wore a silk bathrobe that she had brought with her and her shoulders poked through the thin silk where it clung to her damp skin. Mr. and Mrs. Sprat, he thought. We divide the world between us. It was like he had never been awake before and they were together on this slow Sunday morning, all around them the sounds of leaving, car trunk lids slamming, parents yelling at their children and the children yelling back. They read the paper together and drank their coffee and then June Leaf made more in the little gurgling coffeepot next to the bathroom sink. They could live like this: these interchangeable American lives. Somewhere there was important football, too.

"I wish . . ." June Leaf said.

"What?"

"Nothing," she said. But Winslow knew what she meant, and he wished, too: some other life, some other fate, some other history.

They checked out at their leisure, ten-thirty or eleven. By noon they were enjoying red beer in the Wolf Den Lodge, on the shores of Lake Coeur d'Alene. There were several parties of snowmobilers in there as well in their heavy clothes and boots, drinking draft beer and peppermint schnapps and red-faced in the heat and alcohol. They grouped themselves in circles around the television sets and whooped with pleasure whenever their team—was it the Packers?—scored. Winslow and June Leaf sat at the bar and watched them in the mirror and watched themselves—droopy and dog-faced—in the mirror, the dim bar-light filtering through bottles. Again Winslow found himself longing for that other life. He could be working in the hospital still. He could be ordinary.

On the other hand they did all seem to be idiots, these snow-mobilers. You had to draw the line somewhere. Snowmobilers did not get to have sex with women like June Leaf, tall and slender in the mirror, her long hands lying on the bar like cats, circling, nesting around the base of her glass. Snowmobilers did not read Auden. Maybe one did somewhere but none of these. Bratwurst and penis jokes, Ford versus Chevrolet.

And then the Mint in Wallace, Idaho. Wallace was—or had been once—a town of bars and whores, a place for railroaders and miners to surface for a weekend of sin. Winslow loved it here, although the U & I rooms, the last of the old whorehouses, had shut down a couple of years ago. Also, they had jammed a freeway through the edge of town that was unmissable; when you walked the old streets it was always present at the end of the block, a landing from another planet. Everything ended, Winslow knew that. He just felt it here, a town he heard his father talk about over poker chips when he thought the boy upstairs asleep. . . . They walked the wet streets hand in hand, idling along, looking for the old whorehouses, finding them. Something, rain or snow, was falling out of the dark sky, and every dollar had left town, even the dollars on the Interstate were just passing through at seventy, and the cars that were left were old and rusted and dented and slow.

"I hitchhiked out here when I was seventeen," Winslow said. "I came to get laid."

"And?"

"And nothing," he said. "They told me to come back in a

year. The cops were in on it, everybody was in on it, but they had to run it clean so nobody got in trouble."

"What were they like?"

"Who?"

"The whores."

"I never made it back," Winslow said. "I never made it back before they closed the houses. Eighteen years old and I was in the Army. I can tell you all about Thailand if you want to hear it."

"I don't think I do," said June Leaf.

"I don't think you do, either," Winslow said.

The slow cars, poor people in them, driving by suspiciously. The mines were closed, all of them, and the dead lay underground, the seventy killed in the Sunshine disaster. The tide of money that had inundated Portland, the Lexuses and hot tubs, and stainless-steel refrigerators, had never made it to Wallace, Idaho, would never make it here, poisoned little town. The smelter fumes had killed most of the trees and stunted the ones that lived. Nobody in the Mint Bar had a full set of teeth and nobody would even look at them, the strangers, the rich.

"Railroad whores," June Leaf said, when they were back in the car. "What kind of life is that?"

Winslow knew what she meant, which was not what she was saying. The smell of failure clung to them even in the leather seats of the Lincoln. The poisoned town had poisoned them.

"I don't know," said Winslow. "It didn't seem so bad. It didn't seem horrible."

"Not for the men," June Leaf said.

They were climbing up the Idaho side of the pass and all around them the mountains were white and deep. A forest fire had burned up one side of the canyon and the burnt trees were black and spindly; Switzerland on the other side, pine branches buried in snow.

"A dozen tricks a night," June Leaf said. "Not a lot of pretty girls in there, I imagine. Not a lot of girls who could get along somewhere else."

"I never went back," Winslow said.

"My friend Karen? You met her in San Francisco that once."

Winslow shrugged his shoulders. Friend or girlfriend, there had been a couple of girlfriends for June Leaf, and this Karen person had looked at him with that kind of mistrust. But Winslow hadn't asked, and June Leaf hadn't volunteered.

"Back when she was on heroin Karen would do tricks. She said she liked it when she started, she felt smarter than they were. Then this guy put her in the hospital."

WELCOME TO MONTANA, read the sign at the top of the pass: mud and gravel, big trucks idling, a gray-white landscape dissolving into a gray-white sky. It seemed to Winslow inauspicious.

"I didn't do it," Winslow said.

"You went to the whorehouses."

"In Bangkok."

"It's not your fault," June Leaf said. "It's just a world and you were in it but still it's fucked up."

Winslow didn't say anything. It still shocked him a little to hear a woman curse, though God knows he should have been used to it. Some little thrill of irritation, dislike. They drove in silence, slightly tense, through the mess of melted snow and gravel, the water thrown up by the wheels of passing cars, Winslow with both hands on the wheel and the wipers slapping back and forth. He felt grandfatherly and dumb behind the wheel, his hands planted at two o'clock and ten o'clock, leaning slightly forward, peering through the windshield. He felt old, unlovable. Nobody would ever fuck him again.

Then June Leaf curled toward him in her seat and put her long hand on his thigh. *Tropism*, Winslow thought. It was like having a cat.

Then, farther down the pass, this happened: the clouds broke open and then all the way open and the sun blasted down. It was not like winter sunlight at all but full and strong, he could feel the heat of it even through the window. The snowcovered hills were lit so bright you could barely look at them, and the green trees down by the water shined. Winslow felt his heart lift: sunlight. Maybe this would be all right. He stopped the car at a kind of turnout, he couldn't tell if it was supposed to be a rest stop or what but he could see the river through the trees. He found his felt-lined mukluks in the back seat and pulled on his parka.

"Where are you going?" June Leaf asked.

"I don't know," he said. "Take a look around."

Winslow did know where he was going, though: down to the river. The snow was ankle-deep and hard, breaking under his step as he edged down the riverbank. What if he fell in? The sudden overpowering cold, surrounded by water. But when he got to the river's edge he saw that it was only a few inches deep along the bank and running fast, too fast and bumpy over the rocks for ice to form. The water was clear and the rocks at the bottom were yellow and brown and blue, clean-looking.

Winslow stood there a minute looking at the water running over rocks and then he lit a cigarette and stood there a minute longer. He could feel the sunlight hot on his neck despite the cold. The sunlight. He thought of the fish leading their fish lives down under the ice, the winter's slow swimmers, half alive, swimming in their sleep. He looked up into the brilliance of a clear blue sky and the sunlit exaltation of the white hills and felt himself lucky—just to be there, just to see it. He took the sunlight and the river into himself and carried it with him as he trudged back to the car, got in, started up the Lincoln and drove off toward the 10,000 Silver Dollar Bar. Maybe this would be all right after all. Maybe.

Jack Walrath was a short dapper man with a goatee who looked slightly like the Devil. Maybe he was the Devil. Like every other person in academic life that Winslow had ever met, Walrath seemed anxious to get his side of the story out first.

"I don't know what happened to Cardigan," he said. "He was coming and he was coming and he was coming and then, a month ago, he sends a postcard to say he's not coming. A *postcard*."

"Why not?"

"He won't even answer the phone," Walrath said. He looked around the restaurant to see if there were any spies. "I think it was Belva," he said. "They were in the middle of trying to work something out about housing and she must have said something."

"I thought the apartment was part of the deal," June Leaf said.

"Cardigan had dogs. You can't have dogs in university housing." Walrath looked suddenly at Winslow, alarmed. "You don't have a dog, do you?"

"I don't."

"I should have asked before."

The wait-person—a former student of Walrath's—came by to pour the wine again and to apologize again for the delay. Their entrées would be out in just a minute. It was her fault. She hadn't written the orders down correctly. Did Walrath say that Andrew Cardigan *wasn't* coming?

"You didn't hear?" Walrath told her. "He canceled out right after classes ended last fall. By *postcard.*"

"Wow," the waitress said. "That's going to make some people really mad. Everybody was really looking forward to working with him."

"It wasn't for lack of trying," Walrath said. "I thought we had him all sewn up."

Winslow looked around the fussbudget little dining room, a room he seemed to have disappeared from, and wondered who these Athens intellectuals and bons vivants were. This palace of fine dining. Soft jazz was percolating down from unseen speakers and half the menu was in French but still the customers mainly looked like they were about to go hiking: sweaters and Polarfleece and boots with manly soles. Winslow was one of two men wearing sport jackets in the whole place and the only one wearing it as a uniform; the other man's was muted luxurious wool, a fine-looking thing but more of a statement. There were lots of good teeth and plenty of good hair and a general aura of youth and vigor.

He lifted his glass and drank and noticed, at the same time

Walrath did, that he had nearly emptied his wine in the time Walrath had taken a few small sips.

"What have you been working on lately?" Walrath asked.

"Oh, you know," Winslow said. "This and that."

"I loved that last book," Walrath said.

Winslow wanted to ask him, Which one was that? Because his last book had been published four years before, by a press so completely obscure and financially shaky that Winslow was never sure whether they were in business or not. He had touched the book—had held a copy in his hand—but he had never actually seen one for sale in a bookstore. Even before, when he was still writing, he suffered from commercial leprosy.

But Walrath wouldn't want to hear about it. Everything was fine inside his little bubble. He had found a body to put in the classroom.

Just the thought of all the wasted work that had gone into the project, the typing itself, the sheets of paper filled with foolishness and discarded, the afternoons and evenings in which his excitement kept him awake and slugging at the thought of the next morning's writing—the brilliancies he might uncover there—the accurate and consoling words—the futility of the whole effort came pressing in on him again, and he lifted his glass and drank, until it was empty. Then filled it himself under Walrath's watchful eye.

June Leaf said, "Richard tells me you get good students here. Is that still true?"

"More and more," said Walrath. "Harvard, Princeton, Stanford—they get better every year. It's a mystery to me."

"What part is the mystery?"

"We live in a commercial world," said Walrath. "It's the only denominator we have anymore, success and money. The only way of keeping track. Once upon a time you could be virtuous, or daring, or great. You could even keep score using poetry—look at Keats, never had a nickel, died a happy man, more or less. Now it's all money."

Winslow thought there was nothing worse than hearing an argument you agreed with coming out of the mouth of a man you didn't like. An argument he had made himself, an argument he had *had* with himself.

"These kids," said Walrath, "they come out of these good schools, they know something's wrong but they don't know what."

"And they think that writing poetry's going to fix it," Winslow said.

"They don't know what they're doing," Walrath said. "They're just looking around, trying to find something, I don't know. I hitchhiked across the country twice. It's the same thing."

It must have been showing on Winslow's face, how he felt about this pipsqueak, because June Leaf suddenly darted back into the conversation. "How long have you lived here?" she said. "How did you end up here?"

Walrath turned to her with enthusiasm, eager to get out of Winslow's headlights. Another one afraid to make enemies. He was probably all right, perfectly likable, an academic fixer but so what? Plumbers were out there struggling to get ahead of the next plumber. Everybody was trying to get ahead but Winslow. Everybody wanted what Walrath had, at least this evening: comfort, authority, company, a glass or two of wine and fussy food. Everybody loved food now, everybody but Winslow. It wasn't exactly that he didn't care but he really didn't care. The foods he liked—bacon, butter, onions—were because of the way they smelled when they were cooking, the memories that were carried with the smells: his mother's kitchen, his first little family . . . The same with cars: he didn't really care about cars at all but riding in the big Town Car was just like riding in the big Buicks and Oldsmobiles of his childhood, with the ropes across the back of the seats. Always some gigantic car, hand-me-downs from his mother's rich aunts, who felt sorry for her for marrying beneath her station. They gave little Richard books and paid for his fancy education so he might end up here, begging off this little bearded weasel. All gone now, all dead and dissolving into the Oregon soil.

The arrival of his food snapped Winslow back into the present. June Leaf looked irritated, so he supposed they had noticed he was gone. Well, Winslow thought, fuck them. The waitress poured his glass full again and he drank.

"I love this place," Walrath said. "Just for the inventiveness."

June Leaf looked at him warningly and Winslow didn't say anything. The mess on his plate didn't remind him of anything—except, maybe, that Peter Pan had been at work in the kitchen. His steak was wearing a little party hat of fried onions and there was some kind of vegetable confetti strewn over the plate. He dug in, wishing for the millionth time that he had been born earlier, in the meat-and-potatoes era of American life. There were *peapods* on his plate, with tiny peas still sleeping inside.

"How bad is it going to get?" Winslow asked. "The winter, I mean. I've never spent a winter in the mountains."

"It's not so bad. Put snow tires on your car and buy some long johns. Just make sure you get the synthetic kind and not the cotton ones. It's actually kind of beautiful once you get used to it."

But *beautiful* was not the word for that January night. They came out of the restaurant door and were almost blown back in by the wind. It was hard to say if it was snowing or if it was just the wind, piling up the loose snow and driving it into their faces. They cut short their goodbyes and simply waved at each other, grinning to signify their good intentions. Then Walrath scurried off to his own enormous truck, some Japanese equivalent of a Land Rover that looked like it could climb trees.

Winslow and June Leaf hurried to the Lincoln, expecting to find shelter there. But inside the car was cold as a cave, and at first it didn't want to start. When it did turn over, cold air came blasting out of the heater vents and June Leaf started to laugh.

"Poor you," she said. "Poor Richard! A frozen hell."

"But beautiful," he said. "Don't forget that it's beautiful."

"I saw that right away," she said.

Her words, his breath condensed into a thin ice-fog on the inside of the windshield, which Winslow swiped at with his handkerchief. It froze again instantly.

"I guess we just have to wait for it to warm up," he said.

"I'm freezing."

"I don't think you can drive when you can't see through the windshield. I don't think you're supposed to."

She leaned the armrest up and huddled against him, thin fingers under his parka, seeking his warmth. *Vampirish*, he thought. But she wasn't.

"California," Winslow said. "We'll go back to the apartment, get our crap and go. We can be on the beach in two days."

"I wish we could," she said.

"What?"

"Nothing."

But when she looked up into his face Winslow saw that she was near crying. He felt it then himself: the next thing, the thing they didn't want to talk about. He was a fool to bring it up.

In another minute the windshield cleared and Winslow drove them home in silence except for the whistling wind outside. The streets were empty, gas-station lights shining through the blowing snow, occasional other cars, nobody walking, no leaves on the trees. The court where Winslow's apartment sat in married student housing was empty, although the blue lights of televisions shined from every window but his.

Inside, she opened a bottle of Johnnie Walker and poured herself a drink and sat down in front of the enormous TV and clicked it on. The apartment came furnished and the TV was part of it. She didn't seem to care what Winslow did. He poured a drink himself and settled in next to her on the couch: early American, floral.

"I should just go," she said.

"Stick around."

"I'm going to call the airline and see if I can switch my ticket," she said. "It's just this waiting around. Waiting for the other shoe to drop."

She was right but Winslow didn't care. When June Leaf was gone she would be gone, and he didn't know if either of them had the energy to start again with the other. The thing was that she loved him and he had managed to fuck it up. But Winslow knew he would have plenty of time to think about that when she was gone.

ESPN. *Antiques Roadshow.* Cooking and police chases. Neither of them was used to the TV, and so it was like a new narcotic to them, wandering from channel to channel, never lingering.

"I'm not working," June Leaf said. "I'm not doing anything. I'm just sitting around waiting."

What it reminded Winslow of was his first wife, when she had a miscarriage. It seemed like the end of the world to her, to both of them. They sat in their little house in Gresham and watched television from the time he came home from work until it was time to sleep. For all he knew, Lily might have had it on all day, too. They watched comedies and dramas and cartoons, whatever was on. And it was a blessing, a way to get through the hours. Something like that, it healed invisibly, over time, like a scab knitting together, the new skin growing in from the edges. But you needed something to do with the time.

It seemed so strange to think that June Leaf would one day be a memory, too, a safe remote memory like that baby who never was.

He kissed her and her mouth tasted like whiskey.

"I can feel my brain running out my ears," he said, changing the channel for the third time in five minutes.

"Me, too," she said, and touched his dick through the cloth of his pants. Then changed her mind, shook her head, got up and got the bottle. She set it on the coffee table in front of them.

"Just like home," she said. "We've got everything we need. Cable TV."

"Just like home," he said. He picked the bottle up and filled both their glasses and turned the television off. He could hear the baby next door crying through the thin wallboard, and somebody somewhere having an argument. The wind was curling in the corners of the building, rattling the wires outside, seeping through any tiny crack, the edges of the windows, bottom of the front door. It was warm enough but it wasn't quite warm. They could feel the press of wind, the windblown snow battering softly against the window glass like an attack of moth wings.

June Leaf turned the television back on.

"I don't like it here," she said. "I feel like I'm going to die."

"You're not going to die."

"I'm not going to die *here*," she said, lighting a cigarette. "That Jack Walrath is an awful little man."

"He's not so bad."

"Listen to yourself. You didn't have to watch yourself when we were eating dinner, Richard, making faces at him the whole time. You're fucking *excellent* at that, Richard, a real politician. He'll never guess what you really think of him."

"Have you ever read any of his alleged poetry? It's shit from top to bottom. Talented gibberish."

"Well, we know he's not your favorite," she said. "You don't have any favorites anymore. Everybody you like is dead."

"What are we fighting about?"

"I don't know."

She sipped her scotch and stubbed the cigarette out rudely, then curled away from him on the couch.

"You've got a chance here, maybe," June Leaf said. "You can't be so negative all the time! Nobody's going to do anything for you if they think you hate them."

"You know what they were going to pay Cardigan?"

"What?"

"You know what they were going to pay Cardigan?"

"No, I don't."

"The department secretary gave me the wrong contract at first," Winslow said. "Thirty-seven thousand dollars. For the same semester. Then he disappears and they get me on the cheap."

"I thought you liked Cardigan."

"He can write," Winslow said. "That's not what they're paying him for. They're paying for the English accent and the sweaters and shoes. He elevates the tone."

"What does that have to do with you? You take everything personally, Richard. I mean, a talent-free dickhead like Jeff Koons is out there making millions, does that mean I should stop working? You let things stop you, Richard. You shouldn't let things stop you."

Winslow felt a little breeze blow through him. She knew

about the work. She had to know about the work, of course it all made sense, but this was his secret, the thing he had to hide, his own futility. In his confusion he sipped his drink, looked at the television: a monkey jumping up and down on a table. When he turned back to June Leaf, her face was right there.

She said, "A ceramic statue of Michael fucking Jackson and his monkey. I don't take it personally."

He kissed her again and felt her flat breasts under her silk shirt, like a man's shirt but silk, her tall skinny body.

"I just want to get drunk," she said. "A night like this."

"A night like this," he said, and poured their glasses full again.

The first class was the next day. Winslow spent the hour before class in his cell staring at the first page of the First Elegy. All
those capital letters, Beauty and Terror and Night. What had
seemed a clever idea in his bathtub seemed ruinous now.

Rilke was a German, that was the basic problem. *Many a star
was waiting for you to espy it. . . .* It was also possible that the
translation was not good. Winslow couldn't say for sure. The
only German he knew was from World War II movies and not
much help in the present circumstance: *Achtung!*

Also he was wondering if June Leaf would be there when he
got home. She had still been threatening to change her reservation when he left to trudge over to the campus in the deep soft
snow. A blue-sky day, beautiful, the sunlight hard on the white
snow. All the way over to the school he felt an impulse turning
him back, back toward her. He had a feeling that if he could

just go back to her and find the right words, the exact right words, he could make everything all right again between them.

He also knew, from experience, that there were no such words. But it didn't stop him from wanting to go back to the apartment and try.

Even when he arrived, sitting in his little concrete cell of an office, with the door closed, listening to the bustle of purpose and cross-purpose in the hallway outside and trying to think of something to say about Rilke, he fought the impulse to go back to her. If she was still there. Fought the impulse to call, which was just as well—he had forgotten the new number and forgotten to bring it with him. Also he knew in some kind of existential sense that he just had to go forward and let things turn out however they turned out.

The fucking German, though . . . Winslow puzzled through the opening two pages again to see if he could make sense or beauty or music out of them. No, and again, no. More accurately, not quite, the center of the thing eluding him. He had the sense—a feeling he hated—that the writer knew exactly what he was talking about but could have said it more plainly.

Somebody else's children were playing outside in the snow, throwing halfhearted snowballs at each other that dissolved in midair. Twenty or twenty-two. The baby would have been that old by now. Strange how often he thought about the baby.

The bell rang and it was time to go face the music. The halls all hurry and bustle and wool scarves and the linoleum wet from melted snow, the same smell of wet wool as winter in Oregon; and for a moment Winslow was a boy again, on his way to Communion or to algebra. How many castoff selves he carried inside him.

They were waiting for him in a small airless brick room with a single tiny window and several people's abandoned books and journals in racks along the wall. Linoleum on the floor, fluorescent overhead lights. There were only eight of them around the table, Winslow counted: more girls than boys. Someone must have told them there was something wrong with Winslow.

He threw the *Duino Elegies* down onto the table and sat.

"You're going to have to help me out on this," he said. "I don't understand a goddamned word of it."

They looked at each other, puzzled, wondering whether to be amused or not. They looked clean, intelligent, well rested and well read, and Winslow knew, just looking at them, that he had nothing of value to offer.

"College," he said. "You're having fun here? You like it?"

Stirring and mumbling, a general lack of understanding.

"Never mind," he said. "How do you usually do this?"

"We, uh, read the work? and then we talk about it?"

The ringleader was the tall girl with the odd complexion—some afterlife of earlier face trouble—but the others found it amusing enough. That was all right. Winslow didn't mind amusing them.

"OK," he said. "Who's got what?"

"Nobody's got anything *the first day*," the tall girl said. It was the schoolyard voice, the one burned into him on the playground, telling little Richard that he was retarded.

"What do you want to do, then?" he asked.

"Why are we reading this, anyway?" asked one of the other girls; a drawn, sallow face; a complainer, was Winslow's bet. "I thought this was going to be a workshop."

"Well," Winslow said. And anyone who knew him, anyone who could read his face, would have dropped the matter then and there, would have quickly changed the subject or changed the channel or left the room. But they didn't know him yet, his famous insecurities. The little light went on in his head to tell him he was doing something dangerous but Winslow ignored it.

"Geniuses that you no doubt are," he said. "As your teachers and your parents have told you since time immemorial. I know this can't be true here, but I have noticed in other situations that sometimes even the poets don't read poetry. A baffling turn of events but true. Nobody reads poetry. So just in case, on the off-chance this might happen to be true for one or two of you, we're going to read some Rilke."

Good deal, Winslow told himself. Get the crowd on your side. Make the people happy.

"I thought you didn't like Rilke," said the one girl, the skinny girl, with so many piercings she looked like a change purse jangling. She was pale and blonde and wolfish, wolf eyes, blue and bright.

"I don't understand it," Winslow said. "Not the same thing. Besides, he comes recommended—I figure there's got to be something there somewhere."

"And we're supposed to help you find it."

"Something like that." He pulled the book back toward himself across the table, looked around from face to face and shrugged.

"We'll just have to see how it goes," he said.

They looked at each other and laughed, still nervous, and then back at Winslow.

"That's it?" the tall girl said.

"That's all I've got," he said. "I've got nothing."

"I've got a question," said the girl with the piercings. "What are you doing here? What happened to Andrew Cardigan?"

"Ask your keepers," Winslow said. Then it occurred to him that there had been enough hostility, at least for opening day.

"He disappeared, is what your boy Walrath told me. I suspect there's more to it than that but they wouldn't tell me. I know how much they were going to pay him, though."

A general laugh. Then the piercéd girl said, "How much?"

"Thirty-seven thousand dollars," Winslow said.

A small hush descended on the room; a number apparently too large for the poets to contemplate.

"In the big world it's not much," he said. "Your parents make more."

"My parents are dead," said the piercéd girl.

She said it cool and level like she was reading a line from a poem and then she waited for Winslow to respond, giving away nothing. Staring him down with her wolf eyes.

"I'll see you next week," he said, leaving nothing at all settled. Another fine start. He picked up his copy of the Rilke book like it weighed a hundred pounds and shuffled off toward his little cell, leaving the little stink behind him.

"Excuse me?"

It was the red-haired boy from the class, a big boy with an open, manly face and large hands. Winslow had already noticed his hands, lying on the table like animals, things with a life of their own.

"Can I help you?" Winslow asked.

The boy flushed like Winslow had insulted him but persevered.

"That translation that you're using? I know it's the old one, probably the one you're used to and all. And Spender's great, don't get me wrong, but that translation is kind of a dog."

Winslow stood blinking at him for a moment. Then invited the boy into his office. Dave—his name was Dave—sat in the antique office chair like he was the one who this belonged to and not Winslow, which was probably the truth.

"There are a couple of newer translations," the boy said. "I don't know if they have the poetry of the Spender translation but they're a lot more accurate."

"Poetry schmoetry," Winslow said. "You read German?"

"Enough."

"What is it with the fucking Germans?"

"Hey, you assigned it," Dave said. "I'm just trying to help out."

He looked honest enough, Winslow thought. He wondered how a person named Dave had made it into poetry school. Usually they were named David.

"What's the better translation?"

Dave told him: a twelve-dollar book, and available on the Internet for cheaper. It wouldn't break the bank for anybody. Plus, he said, it wouldn't be bad to have both translations to look at, you could learn something from comparing them.

"Well, all right, then," Winslow said. "Pass the word. We'll read both of them, and see if this makes any sense in stereo. Thank you."

"No," Dave said, suddenly red-faced again. "No, thanks for considering it. I'm really looking forward to this class."

Then looked at his shoes, then rousted himself to his feet and out into the corridor. One last thing: he turned back into the office.

"I'm a great admirer of your work," he said. "A lot of us are. I'm really glad you came."

Then fled, and left Winslow alone again in his office, feeling like a thief. It wasn't that he didn't want to. Maybe he really did have something to say to them. He did, in fact, have something to say, but it wasn't anything they wanted to hear: the thousands of pages of wasted words, years of heart and soul and discipline for what? Ships in bottles, one after another.

Maybe they could do what Winslow had not been able to. Maybe they could make a difference. He could help them try. He was going to have to get through the next few months somehow. He could help them try.

Although these were his listed office hours Winslow packed up his satchel and left. He couldn't sit still and there was nothing for him here. He put his businessman's shoes in his satchel and wore the felt-lined mukluks which an ex-Alaskan at Kelly's had loaned to him, or given him, it wasn't clear. The ex-Alaskan swore he was never going back to anywhere he might need them. Winslow's giant parka slid over his sport jacket, the synthetic-wolf-fur ruff tickling his ears. He had rarely felt more ridiculous than he did in this getup. He looked like he was about to go exploring for oil on the North Slope.

And of course the piercéd girl was waiting in the hall outside his office, about to knock.

"Come on in," he said. "I was just about to . . ."

The blonde and piercéd girl looked him up and down with her blue wolf-eyes, as if not quite certain of what she saw. Then she shook her head and walked past him into the office. Sweating already, Winslow followed her in.

"I just wanted to say that I don't give a shit about Cardigan," she said.

She waited for him to say something then but Winslow couldn't think of what. She seemed to be furious about something.

"What's your name?"

"Marie of Roumania," she said.

"What?"

"Erika," she said. "Erika Jones."

"And love is a thing that can never go wrong."

A little head-fake from Erika to show she approved, a little shake that set all the hardware in her ears to swaying. She also had a tattoo on her neck, fingering its way out of the collar of her ratty sweater.

She said, "It probably sounded like it was some big disappointment when we found out Cardigan wasn't coming but really I don't think he can write. Do you?"

"I don't know," he said. "I haven't read all of it. He's got a really good reputation as a teacher, too, from what I've heard."

"Come on."

"He's all right," Winslow said. "He's not my favorite but he's all right. Is that what you were looking for?"

"Thank you," said Erika. "Anyway . . ."

"We aim to please," Winslow said.

She looked up angrily—though Winslow couldn't tell what he had done—and bolted, leaving him in his Eskimo duds and sweating. Winslow wondered what he had just seen. Had she really been angry? A clumsy girl but still. Something. He closed his office door behind himself and realized that he had left his satchel inside. Then decided, empty-handed, to leave as he was. He wouldn't need anything. He'd leave Rilke alone for tonight.

He walked home through an afternoon of such startling brilliance and clarity that it was like walking through a diamond, bright sun on glittering snow and blue skies above. Civic virtue expressed itself in the form of neatly plowed sidewalks and driveways. Apart from an occasional awkward moment crossing the curb or maneuvering across the berm that the plow had thrown up, it was an easy and pleasant twenty-minute walk, and mothers with their children in strollers smiled at him, and told him what a nice day it was.

Winslow walked through this wintry brilliance like a man who has forgotten something crucial, a birthday, an appointment. . . . He couldn't tell what was weighing on him. June Leaf, maybe. The piercéd girl's anger. Maybe it was this: the way that feminine anger followed him around, and Winslow's certainty that they were right, all the women were right, they should have been angry with him.

Maybe it was something else. He couldn't tell.

June Leaf was gone when he got back to the apartment.

RICHARD, said the note on the kitchen table. He opened it greedily, hoping for—what?—for drama, words that could not be taken back, revelations, surprises, secrets. He longed for opera and got a laundry list: *I have changed my reservations and I will be seeing you again in March. Keep warm and take care of yourself. I love you June Leaf* (the awkwardness of the painter in print was one of the things he loved about her).

He had been right all along.

He lit a cigarette. The refrigerator ticked on in the stillness of the kitchen. Outside, three o'clock, the children were all home from school and racketing around in the snow. Beautiful and optimistic young mothers bundled their babies in layers of fleece and went walking, even running around the golf course, even skiing in their grownup baby clothes with the real babies swaddled into backpacks behind them, red-faced in the cold air. This was not a good place for Winslow. His own kind were elsewhere.

Winslow went to the river, a place that Forager—a friendly face in the English department—had told him about, south of town. His fishing crap was all in a duffel in the trunk of the Town Car and Winslow set out just as he was, parka and all. Parka, mukluk, kayak, what else? Kodak, maybe. Chinook. He drove out through the brilliant afternoon and knew that he would be too late when he got to the river but it would be better than the married students' apartment. Cars and semis and gigantic pickup trucks with dual wheels in the back and mustaches to match, even the cars looked nothing like Oregon. Fine with Winslow. He didn't miss the little Euro jelly beans in all their bright colors, or else the sedate Mercedes, the restrained Volvo dressed in earth tones. . . . Here the earth tones came from dirt, a winter's worth of gravel spray up the side of every vehicle. Even the cars were poor and dirty.

He parked along the side of the road and dressed in his fisherman's motley: a sweater, another sweater, a red nylon windbreaker with the name of a bar in Oregon City on the back. He pulled his neoprene waders—size Medium King—over pants and all, and then the silly vest and wool watch cap and half-finger gloves. His fingers were sluggish in the cold trying to string up his rod. The heat was ebbing from the afternoon although the sunlight was still holding on by the water. Finally he was rigged up and ready. Across the railroad tracks and down the bank and across a little iced-over side channel Winslow crunched through the snow. It was amazing, always, the heat inside the rubber waders and the frozen cold outside. He could feel the cold everywhere around him but it couldn't touch him, not in his silly space suit.

The river was running slow with a little smoke coming off it in the cold air. He found a spot along the gravel bank where the water was running clear and eased his way out into the current. The bottom of the river was coarse gravel of every muted color and the water was running gently, easy walking in his felt-soled boots. Nothing was rising but there was a hatch of midges over the water, black specks circling and darting in the clear cold air. Winslow tied on the smallest fly in his box with numb unsteady hands, stabbing at the tiny eye of the tiny hook with the end of the hair-thin tippet. Then remembered—he always forgot at first—the Tom Sawyer trick: hold the tippet steady and bring the eye of the hook to it. He tied the microscopic knot and cast his first cast into a Montana river.

The line tumbled out over the water like a bag of wet laundry and landed in a puddle not far from his feet. The swift dark shadows under the water were the fish he had scared with his ugly cast, running for Venezuela. The water in the line, as he drew it in to cast again, froze his fingers right away and Winslow saw that this, too, was another foolish errand. Nothing good would happen here.

He drew his line back anyway and cast again and this one was better. The line sailed out a little ways and the fly landed plausibly, a little heavy for such a tiny fly but passable. He let the fly drift down, although he knew that the fish had all departed with his original cast. Again and again he cast over the water, until he began to feel graceful. Like starting up an old machine, the timing and feel were there in his arm but he had to turn it over a few times to find it. When he felt like he could make it go, Winslow moved up the bank, moving slow and quiet as he could, shuffling his feet on the underwater gravel. He took up his new station and cast upstream—a decent cast—and let the fly drift down and *now*, he thought, there's a fish *right there*. And as he realized that there was no fish there, at all, as he relaxed and prepared to take up line for the next cast, a bit of gravel bottom disengaged itself and rose up toward the surface and became a fish at the moment that it sipped the fly.

Winslow reared back with all his might and lifted the tiny trout out of the water bodily: a nine-inch rainbow and surprised as hell. With trembling fingers Winslow held the slim body, working fish slime into the wool of his gloves and removing, with his surgical forceps, the tiny hook from the delicate mouth. The red band running down the side of its body and the dark spots. He let it go and watched it disappear, become part of the water again, and then some small thing was better inside him. The sun was off the water now, and his hands were cold. He turned and started toward the car. June Leaf was gone, and he was left behind. But all that night, all through the drunken sleep punctuated with alarms and starts, he remembered: the slim bright body of the rainbow as it swam away from him, the arc of the line as it came off his rod, the state of grace.

Winslow wondered where it would end this time. The first time was in Hawaii, when he was twenty-three. Winslow could still remember the night perfectly, although he still couldn't tell what any of it meant. He had been driving an army-soldier-green Impala back along the coast road in Oahu when it was still a two-lane road. For someone from Oregon it was a strange night: dripping rain and greenery inching up to the sides of the road, nearly brushing the sides of the car in places, the dense dripping foliage of the Coast Range but when he rolled down the window the air was warm and thick and fragrant with the odor of tropical rot.

Winslow was drunk on Army time, which was not going to end well. He had authorization for the car but he was going to have to get back onto the base somehow. Which was just a problem, not the real problem. The real problem did not have a name.

He might end up back in Vietnam, which was part of it. But really it was something else. He was drunk and he remembered that he had felt like he could see his own life whole, like he was flying above himself, looking down at himself. He always knew there was something wrong with him but this was just one night where he could see it clearly: he was broken, he was born broken, he wasn't going to get any better. Even now, looking back, he wasn't sure he disagreed. But that night with the moon coming in and out of the heavy trees and shining across the windshield was the first time it had come to him and it came as a certainty. Like a punch in the stomach it could not be denied. The moon was flickering in and out and the ocean would sometimes flash into view down over his right side, the waves breaking white in the moonlight. It was like he would be fine if he didn't have to stop driving. He could just keep going and everything would be fine. The Impala was a fine big car although low on amenities. He had cigarettes and a pint of Southern Comfort, he shuddered to think of it now but Southern Comfort, he could still taste the sweet sticky burn if he thought about it.

Then, going sixty, he turned the wheel an inch and the car rammed into the concrete base of a tunnel entrance.

Slowly the car folded around the sharp edge of the concrete and slowly the steering wheel came toward his chest with a beautiful rending sound of metal on metal.

He woke up in the hospital. It took less time to do than it does to tell about it. They asked him over and over but Winslow never came up with an answer that satisfied anybody: just an inch, the work of one finger. He didn't know himself, except that it still and always made some kind of sense, it fit together in some way he couldn't explain: driving at night, drinking, going nowhere. . . .

The Army docs didn't like any of this. They were used to naked aggression, hillbilly psychopaths, sudden flipouts, knives and guns. Winslow with his quiet little problem was a mystery to them and an unattractive one. They put him on the ward with Jimmy Kipp, who couldn't stop fighting, a Blackfeet Indian from Montana who looked like he came straight off the nickel. They put him in with a boy from Texas who claimed he was Bo Diddley's son. Apparently they were hoping one of them would kill Winslow and put an end to the mystery but they were all mysteriously kind to him. The doctors never did figure out what was wrong with him beyond the broken ribs and facial bruising.

The second time was quieter. He lay down on his couch in Gresham and didn't get up.

This was at the end of that particular life. He had been honorably discharged, which always made him think of an infection, and then spent four years drinking on the GI Bill as an English major. He met a girl and married her. He published his first four poems and got a job in the hospital to tide them over until he was famous. Fueled by a hot, unreasonable optimism, they bought a house and made detailed plans for future happiness. She was a nurse, she liked pills, she didn't mind bringing a few home for Winslow once in a while. But nothing dangerous, nothing out of control—just a few white crosses on a Saturday night, a couple of APCs on Sunday morning to ease the pain. A fool's paradise, it seemed to Winslow, but the only kind of paradise that would let him in.

It would have worked, too. It should have worked. He loved her.

It was easy to say that the drinking did them in, and maybe

it did. God knows they did enough drinking. It never occurred to either one of them that it was sad drinking or tragic drinking or symptomatic drinking, though—it was fun, it felt like fun, staying up till *Modern Farmer* came on the TV at five o'clock Saturday morning, driving out to Cannon Beach to watch the sunrise and getting all the way there before any of the five of them remembered that the sun actually rose on the other coast. They went places: Vegas, Hawaii, Mexico. They drank Blue Hawaiis in the same bar Elvis drank them in on Kauai and the curaçao turned their tongues blue. Lily—her name was Lily, dark hair and an open, practical face—had a sister who was a stewardess and they got free tickets all the time: Rome, Orlando, Montreal.

They had friends, too, friends who liked to drink and drive and go places.

In the end it was all Winslow's fault. Looking back, it was as inexplicable as it had been at the time. Something just clicked off in his head one day and the fun went out of it. He went through the motions for a year, hoping that it would all seem like a good idea again, but it felt silly and inconsequential—living for fun, for pleasure and nothing more. To drive three hours for a bowl of clam chowder and a glimpse of a rainy sea felt silly to him, especially when the road led through the damp decaying towns that Winslow really belonged to. He knew what these cars looked like as they passed by, expensive cars with Portland dealership names. All the time he was a kid he told himself that he would end up in one of those cars speeding toward the beach, speeding through the wet green hills like they weren't there, didn't matter. But when he got to that place in his life, it didn't feel right.

He slowed and slowed again. He let the others go without him. He started watching television, sports and old movies, whatever was on, drinking beer and getting fat and watching television. They never talked about it, and when Lily had her miscarriage she joined him on the couch in some kind of wordless, perfect union. They were there together for the last time.

Because when Lily got better she left—left Winslow by himself on the couch. At first she was just gone with their friends, the ones that had been both their friends when Winslow was up and about. But after a while it was one special friend, and Winslow didn't blame her: a photographer and house-painter named Dale with a pleasant Southern accent and winning ways. Winslow did not have winning ways at that point. Winslow was just a fat man on the couch who only shaved when it was time to go to work. This was when he started going to bed early, so Lily wouldn't have to look at him when she got home. Only in the secret hours before daylight was he alive, writing, musing, talking to himself.

Even years later, though, it seemed to Winslow that he was somehow right: that other life was not for him. He was not born to be happy or carefree or careless. It seemed so little to live for, the pleasures of the moment, the adventures. Winslow wanted something more solid to build his house upon, and if—twenty years later—he still had not found it, this did not mean that it was not worth looking for.

He knew he was probably wrong about this.

What happened in the end was one day he just stopped: he didn't get up, didn't shave, didn't get any farther than the refrigerator, where he got himself a nice glass of wine to go with his Frosted Flakes. Lily didn't know that he had been up since five, that he had already made an important and momentous discovery about the series of poems he had been working on, namely that it was all shit.

He was still there when she got home from work, still there when she went out for her date with Dale, asleep on the couch when she got home, drinking wine again when she got up. He went out during the day, while she was gone, for wine, but he did not bathe and he did not shave. He began to hear her on the telephone, talking about him in the third person. She asked everybody what to do with him and everybody had an opinion. In the end Lily called a Cabulance, is what it was called, a lovely word in Winslow's opinion: Cabulance. The Spanish-speaking driver and his helper came in with a wheelchair and loaded Winslow onto it and drove him to Salem, to the state hospital there. "You've Got a Friend" by Carole King played at least twice on the radio on the way down. This was the only detail Winslow could salvage, as they gave him electroconvulsive therapy just after that.

The ECT made him better. They kept him three months to make sure but he was better—livelier, he kept himself occupied and went out of his way to smile and please. He made friends. His special friend was a fellow depressive from Eugene who looked like Winslow's father; he favored the same Pendleton plaid shirts, the same pink-cheeked outdoorsmanship. His name was Nelson Brightwater and he was an avid steelheader, the only thing in all of life he could summon any enthusiasm for. Winslow and Nelson Brightwater would sit by the big windows in the day room and talk about rivers, tactics, anecdotes involving moose and emergency brakes and trips to the emergency room. The sun coming through the big windows felt bright and hot all winter; Winslow could still remember it on the skin of his arms. They talked about fly-fishing for trout on the Deschutes and bait-casting for steelhead on the Alsea, the Coquille, the Necanicum. At some point Nelson Brightwater's daughter brought a portable fly-tying bench to the hospital and he taught Winslow how to tie a few simple, useful patterns: a Prince, a Royal Wulff, a Parachute Adams.

Later Nelson Brightwater shot himself in the mouth with a .38 and lived six weeks, which was hard to think about. Winslow still had the patterns in his head, though, and somewhere in the basement of June Leaf's apartment building he had Nelson Brightwater's portable bench, and every couple of years he would tie up a few and Nelson Brightwater would live in the instructions he had given thirty years ago: how to use the hair stacker, how to keep the hair ends even and neat, how to make a whip finish.

The central thing that Winslow could remember from this time was the feeling of satisfaction he had, all the ride down with Carole King for company. As far as he could take it. As far as he could go. Something at least would happen next and this part would be over. He could feel the same movement starting up inside him, the same gathering wave, and wondered where it would leave him this time. Nothing to do, though. Nothing to do but wait and see.

"*But hark, the suspiration,*" Winslow said, "*the uninterrupted news that grows out of silence.* You know what I think?"

He looked around the room from face to face and clearly they didn't. That early moment in the semester when they were pricing him, trying to see if they would get their money's worth. I will give you my performance, Winslow thought. Then we will go out for drinks.

"This is a poem without a body," he said. "A series of poems. There's no belly here or breast or dick. It's all out of his mind."

They considered this. At least they were thinking. Winslow noticed, just to himself, that he was considering the piercéd girl first, this Erika Jones. She had that light in her eyes, ready to argue. Winslow was ready for a fight. While the class was thinking, he speculated on her breasts; not much, at best. Maybe nothing at all. It was hard to tell, under the ratty sweater.

"Professor Winslow?" Erika Jones asked. "Why does everything have to have a dick?"

"You never noticed that?" said Winslow. "Eliot was a tall thin man and he wrote tall thin poetry. Everything comes out of the body. Look at W. C. Williams, look at Roethke, none of that fussbudget elegance, no linen handkerchiefs. You want a nice fat generous line, go to a fat man."

"That's not true," said the tall girl. "That's not true at all."

"You want truth, go find a thin man," Winslow said. "You want Truth, Beauty, Angels, you need to find a thin man to give them to you. Look at Yeats, wasted half his life on the wacka-wacka when he could have been looking at the world around him. That's what bothers me about this stuff"—and here he let the volume of Rilke fall to the table—"it gives me the vapors, all this truth-and-beauty stuff. Nobody but a thin man could have written it. I'll tell you something else."

They were all looking a little stunned, but the tall girl—the apparent spokesman—summoned herself to ask, "What?"

"This man never had a child," he said. "He never had a child die on him, anyway. All this moonshine about the young dead and how great they are and so forth, he doesn't know what he's talking about. Dead children are all about suffering. I mean a miscarriage is as close as I've ever gotten and it was close enough, I still think about it. Not a week goes by."

A longish silence filled the room and Winslow sat back with some measure of satisfaction. He wasn't there to live down to their expectations.

"Well, so what?" Dave finally said. "Everything has to be written on the body? Out of the body?"

"It's just experience," Winslow said. "He doesn't value the experience, it's all, I don't know, metaphor. But dead babies aren't metaphors. Look, I'm not going to tell you right from wrong—you like this, go ahead and like it, you think it's beautiful, that's fine with me. I'm just going to tell you what makes sense to me, because that's all I know. I don't know what's good and beautiful and all the rest of it. I don't know! I'm not holding out on you. I would tell you if I knew."

A general sigh. He had brought them to the point of confusion, too many lines of thought, too many arrows in too many directions. My specialty, he thought: confusion.

"Then why are we reading this?" asked the tall girl.

"I don't know," Winslow said. "You want to hear me talk about things I understand? It would bore the crap out of you."

"In other words," Erika said, "we're paying you so we can explain it to you?"

"That's close enough," he said. "Look out the window," he said, and they all did: white hell in the afternoon, windblown snow going by like a carnival ride.

"What else are we going to do?" Winslow said. "It's cold outside. It's warm in here. We can sit around and talk about this German fellow and nobody's going to get hurt, maybe somebody will have an idea, maybe I'll even have an idea. OK?"

A general small noise. He had them.

"OK," he said. "So, if you like this, what do you like about it?"

"Liar, liar," Erika said.

Surprised in the act of packing up his satchel, he turned to find her in his office doorway. "What did I do this time?" he said.

"You know exactly what you're doing," she said. "Let's go get a drink, you want to?"

Winslow looked dubiously outside the window, where the afternoon was already gone, a windblown snowy dark.

"I don't know," he said.

"Come on, it's not that bad. You've got to leave the building anyway, unless you were planning to sleep here."

Just the sight of her was exhausting, Winslow thought: those blue eyes, those multiple earrings, that little diamond glittering in her nose. She wore one of those sweaters that only girl poets seemed to wear, brown, baggy and shapeless, oatmeal-colored, frayed. It was impossible to find the shape of her body in the bag of a sweater, but her neck, her wrists were fine and slim. But it was the shine and sparkle in her eyes that scared him, the secret certainty that women seemed to get around Winslow: they knew better, they were all one step ahead of him.

"Come on in," he said. "Close the door."

She looked surprised but went along with him. Winslow unwrapped the scarf from around his neck and undid the parka and sat down in his sport jacket and white shirt behind the desk and took the bottle of Johnnie Walker from the desk drawer.

"Pull up a chair," he said, letting down the venetian blind.

Erika was not often told what to do apparently, but she sat or slouched in the visitor's chair on the other side of the desk. Winslow snapped the desk light on and gestured for her to shut the overhead fluorescents off, which she did. In the yellow incandescent light, in the dark snowy evening, the office was almost pleasant. The walls were lined with bookshelves full of some previous visitor's files and memorabilia, a few books, a few back issues of *Prairie Schooner* and *Black Warrior Review* and *Story*. Winslow found a paper cup and then another in the bottom drawer and poured them each a nice stiff drink.

"Cheers," he said, and they touched paper cups and drank.

Erika shuddered a little at the aftertaste, which gave Winslow an obscure satisfaction.

"Who are these people?" Winslow asked.

"Which people? The ones in the workshop?"

Winslow nodded.

"They're not people at all, they're graduate students, there's a difference. They fuck like bunnies and drink like fish and stay up late worrying that somebody somewhere is getting something that they're not getting."

"It's a good thing you're not like that."

"I'm the worst of them all," she said, slugging down the whiskey in one gulp and putting her empty cup in front of Winslow for more. The worst of what, he wondered: the bunnies or the fish? He poured her glass half full again and settled back, listening to the wind outside.

"Where did you come from?" he asked.

"Which planet, you mean?"

"I don't mean anything of the kind."

"California," she said. "I'm one of those."

"What part of California?"

"The worst part," she said. "I'm not just from California, I'm from *southern* California, and I'm not just from southern California, I'm from Irvine, which is the worst. Ask anybody."

"I always think Los Angeles is supposed to be awful," he said. "Growing up in Oregon, that's all you heard, was how terrible Los Angeles was, and San Diego, too. But every time I go there I like it."

"We *dreamt* about Los Angeles," she said. "We went there twice a year. We went to the beach twice a year. We went to the mall every day. You're expecting me to say I hated it."

"I don't know what to expect out of you," Winslow said, and sipped his drink.

"Nobody was keeping track," she said. "Nobody was keeping score. Everybody's parents were at work or at the gym or doing whatever they did, it was kind of perfect. People doing heroin in the high-school bathrooms."

She was trying to impress him, he could feel it. And while he was not particularly impressed with her daring and recklessness, as he was supposed to be, he was nevertheless flattered that she would even try. More whiskey, Winslow thought: whiskey and the windblown snow outside and the yellow light. He thought then of the kitchen in his rented home: clean, bright, empty.

"How did you end up here?" he asked.

"I went to college," she said. "Three times. The third time it stuck. And I just started writing because, I don't know, the same as anybody else, I guess. Because I thought I was good at it, you know? Because I *knew* I was. Better than the rest of them, anyway."

"That's a nice way of putting it."

"You're not? You don't think that?"

Winslow thought of how he had been, coming home from the service: all alone in the poetry class and scared shitless. Him and the hippies and the girls. The girls were why he stayed at first but he probably shouldn't tell that to her.

"It wasn't hard," he said. "The high school I went to, you were considered an intellectual if you just showed up. Everybody else was out in the parking lot working on their Chevelles."

"Same thing," she said. "Where was that?"

"St. Helens, Oregon," he said, "1964 through 1968. Another world entirely."

"Were you popular?"

"Malaria was more popular than I was," Winslow said. "Death by drowning. The fat boy does not have fun."

He said it lightly but he felt a touch of the old anger rise inside his chest, the permanent anger of the injured child. Staring into his cup of whiskey, he remembered: the Halloween they egged him on his candy rounds, etc. He drained his cup and looked up and she was staring at him with her wolf eyes.

"Nobody has fun," she said.

"They all had more than I did," Winslow said. "It's all water under the bridge now, as my grandmother used to say."

"Let's go out for a drink somewhere," she said. "Don't you want to?"

"Not right now," he said—and knew exactly as he said it that he was mistaken. In fact, that was exactly what he wanted to do: go out someplace pleasant and not too well lit and have several drinks with Erika Jones. He wasn't sure why this was the case but it seemed to be so. But he had already said no.

"Maybe another time," he said.

"No, that's fine," Erika said, disappointed. "I've got to go to work in a little while anyway."

"What do you do?"

"I'm a bartender," she said. "Bartender in a rock club. Silliest job in the world."

She flung herself out of the chair with a sudden violence that surprised him as he was putting the bottle away. She looked around the tiny room as Winslow rose, looked around like she had just landed there by accident.

"This is truly crummy," she said.

Winslow switched on the overhead fluorescent and the room snapped into blue, flickery presence, the cozy lamplit room of a moment ago entirely vanished. He gathered himself and shut everything off and followed Erika out into the hall. The chair of the department, the hefty Belva, was walking down the hall exactly as they came out, together, from the door which had been closed all the way.

Belva scowled at Winslow first and then at the girl. "It's a cold night out there," she said. "Bundle up."

"*Dear Daddy*" was the title of Erika Jones's poem and *Daddy* was the first word and for several minutes Winslow didn't get any farther than that. He sat at his kitchen table, under the bright lights, with a glass of scotch on the rocks and his careful ashtray full of Tareyton butts all lined up in a row and he thought of all the different awful possibilities of such a title.

First of all, of course, was borrowed bile from Plath, a likely outcome. This was what had stopped Winslow in his tracks: an attitude, a mode of writing which he thought he had safely out-grown, but maybe it had been dormant long enough; maybe Plath was coming back again. If anyone would revive her, it would be someone like Erika. Piercings, tattoos, suicide. Taste-less references to the Holocaust would be right up her alley.

The other possibility was maybe worse but Erika didn't seem like a ginger-ale-and-puppies kind of a girl. No: Daddy was going to get it, definitely. His controlling anger, his mindless force, the way he loomed over her childhood like an intermittently erupting volcano, periodically drowning her small cities in ash and fire, Winslow had seen it all the first time and knew that he had lived long enough that he would have to go through it again. He fortified himself with a fresh slug of Black & White before he plunged ahead.

Not bad, he thought.

Surprisingly, not bad.

He read it again, more carefully this time. It was actually fairly good. The anger was there all right—*you walked into the room with your wrecking ball swaying*—but also a mitigating sympathy, a kind of understanding, a look back at the self that was writing. Mysterious, he thought: that quality of authority, it was either there from the first line or it wasn't there at all.

He set the poem aside and went back to the work of the others, preparing for the next day's class. They were disheartening as ever: solid, clever, intelligent, false. It was the absence of failure that Winslow didn't like. An apprentice poem should go fifty feet straight up in the air and explode, it should never ever come down in one piece, it should never politely lie there on the ground, waiting for somebody to come along and pet it. According to Winslow. He lit another cigarette and forged onward through another thicket, a cluster of words around the idea, he suspected, of loss. If you took death and dying out of the lexicon there would be next to nothing left, a little fucking and a few wildflowers. There were times when this felt like work—the attempts to find something constructive to say to little Jenny or Joanie or Johnny about their special little turd-on-a-page which they had specially laid all by themselves.

Apparently Winslow was in a bad mood.

And what did he know, anyway? Why did it matter to anyone what he thought? Assuming, not the best assumption, that anybody did. It's true it was unpleasant work, this being nice about substandard poetry, and work he was not well suited for. But nobody had offered him any other job. And nobody was getting hurt.

Winslow soldiered on. It was his idea that he was living in one of history's flat spots, a time in which nothing much was happening, no particular ideas, no energy. In some sense this was all right with him. Winslow had lived through the seventies in a shirt and tie, holding down a job at the hospital, and really he hadn't gotten much out of the deal except permission to take drugs, which he had already gotten in the Army. And most of those ideas, which had seemed so attractive to so many people, had turned out to be bad ones. Still there were times when the drab nature of the present day seemed depressing to him. So little glory, so little risk, Auden the Hollywood homosexual and the Protestant Yeats in Ireland looking down from a great height at the anthill below. Winslow poured himself another drink: King Ant. I tell the other ants what to do, he thought, while Ezra Pound looks down from heaven laughing. I don't give a rat's ass about your dog who died. It might be better if you left it alone.

He got up and noticed, standing, that he was drunk. He pissed and then watched television for three minutes: restless, restless.

The unfinished manuscripts sat waiting for him at the kitchen table. They would not be any easier sober. He launched back in for a moment and then got stuck in the middle of somebody's little mud puddle and started to wonder if Erika's poem was really as good as he remembered it and went back to take a look.

Even on second reading it seemed all right. Better than all right. Second reading was where things usually fell apart, and he could see the clumsy moments, the stresses that fell in the middle of nowhere, the almost-right words and images calling attention to themselves like peacocks, and in the end he supposed it was actually a fairly bad poem and not even worth revising, was his guess. But it was a bad *real* poem. The writer had something to say and the means to say it. Plus what? Something. That was one thing that Winslow knew about himself: he could tell the difference, he *knew*. And just then he knew—it came to him all at once—that this Erika Jones was, or could be, the real thing.

This felt like a ridiculous thing to think. The real what? The genuine self-deluded article, the best little buggy-whip in all of Montana. If he was any friend to her, he'd tell her to drop it, get a husband and a nice little ranch somewhere. Nevertheless he felt a small sick excitement rise in his chest, an *inkling* is what it was: maybe she was the one. Maybe this girl could make sense out of this. Winslow believed without believing. He did want to see her again, though.

"What *exactly* *were* you doing with our girl Erika?" asked Belva the department chair.

This was at the faculty party, a week later. Winslow had been driven here by the epic boredom of his apartment but now he was trapped in the kitchen and feeling like he was on his way to the principal's office.

"We were talking," he said.

Belva eyed him suspiciously. "About what?"

"About you," Winslow said, and for a quarter of a second she believed him.

"No," he said. "We were talking about angels."

"I'm not an angel?"

"Not in the Rilkean sense," he said. It was something, being flirted with by Belva. It was like getting sexy with a gas pump, he thought, allowing for the fact that he was not perfect himself, not small or lithe or graceful or even, at this point, sober.

"Did she tell you her story?" Belva asked.

"I don't think so."

"She tells everyone her story, but it always changes a little. She gets attention, doesn't she?"

"What is her story?"

"She's not faking," Belva said. She leveled her head at Winslow, a deep, significant look that ordered him to pay attention. "She comes by it naturally. Her mother—I guess she was quite a piece of work. Tried to kill herself several times, said she was going to take Erika with her, just one of those people who never had a day of peace in their lives."

"She said her parents were dead."

"The mother is," said Belva. "She killed herself just as Erika was starting here. I don't know where her real father is—the story is that she came over from Poland with her mother when she was six months old, just the two of them. I guess there's a stepfather around somewhere."

She sipped her glass of gin and then shot Winslow a warning glance and only then did he realize that he had been a little too interested in Erika Jones.

"Smarter than your average bear, is Erika," Belva said. "But nuts. As I'm sure you noticed."

"I don't really keep score," Winslow said.

"Oh, but you do—everybody does, consciously or not. There's just something about a girl like Erika."

"She can write," Winslow said.

"You know what I mean," Belva said. "A girl like that, a little off-kilter, she just seems to draw people in. I don't know—maybe it's just that we get bored with our own lives, you know? A little too safe, a little predictable. And then somebody comes along who really seems like she's ready to take her chances, ready to risk it all, that's attractive. At first. A kind of moth-and-flame effect. She drinks, you know."

Winslow waved around the room with his half-empty glass. "Good thing she's the only one," he said.

"Not like that," Belva said. "Not like you and me. She scares me. She showed up in my office at eleven o'clock one morning and she couldn't stand up. Literally couldn't."

"I'll keep an eye out for her," Winslow said.

"It's not her I'm worried about," Belva said. "She's got people to watch out for her. People care about her."

I get it, I get it, I get it, Winslow thought. What did he have to do to prove it? Put up a banner?

"You have a lovely house," he said.

Belva laughed at that. "I do," she said, "I have a very nice house and I enjoy it very much, as does my husband, Earl. You take care of yourself."

"I will if I can," Winslow said.

"I have no idea what you mean by that," Belva said, and shoved off into the crowd around the hors d'oeuvre table, leaving Winslow in the kitchen with a glass in his hand. He looked around and nobody was smoking, not inside. Seattle had claimed this territory for its own: no smoking, no drinking, no red meat. Although in fairness it did seem like everyone at the department party was doing their best at the liquor cabinet.

Winslow emparka'd himself, patting his pocket to make sure his Tareytons were in it, and went out into the still, cold evening. Snow stood on the ground outside, six inches deep. A solitary hooded figure stood under the eaves, cigarette in hand, smoke swirling through the frozen patio light. Winslow lit up.

She—it was a woman—perked up at the sound of the lighter

and Winslow caught her face It was one of the woman professors, he hadn't sorted out the names yet and he suspected he wouldn't—the dark-haired one with the volatile face. She seemed to be deciding whether to come over to where Winslow stood or not, deciding for several seconds longer than such a decision ought to take. Pretty but nervous-looking, anxious-looking. Maybe forty, maybe older. All this from memory and a single glimpse; she held her face away.

Then decided, and came over to where he stood and lowered her face to him, pretty but anxious, another tall one.

"You're the poet," she said.

"I'm not the only one," he said.

"*Very* funny," she said. "Excellent. Richard Winslow, right?"

He dipped his head. "And you are?"

"Laurie Fletch," she said, extending her hand, which was long and somewhat bony and very cold. Winslow, still warm from inside, felt an impulse to warm her hands in his, an impulse to protect her.

"You moved here voluntarily in the winter," she said, pointing out the snow around them—the snow still falling slowly out of a low, dark sky—with the end of her cigarette. She said, "You must have been fairly desperate."

Winslow was not anxious to talk about this. He said, "What's your field?"

She laughed. "You don't care," she said. "It's like saying, What's your major?"

"You're right," he said. "It is polite meaningless noise, meant to reassure you that I have no ill intentions. What were you hoping for?"

"No more than that," she said. "I teach the twentieth century."

"All of it?"

"Europe, mostly," she said; quickly, almost furtively tossing her old cigarette into the snow and then lighting another. She said, "The people I like, the people I teach, the Nazis killed half of them and Stalin killed the other half. That's not exactly true. Some of them died young on their own and Walser, Walser lived till seventy-something, though he spent the last thirty years in a mental institution."

Winslow wondered if there was some kind of word out—if there had been a meeting on the subject—that everybody had to say the word *crazy* or *mental institution* when he was around. Though nervous Laurie looked like she might be acquainted with the psychiatric arts.

Winslow felt the scotch building up in him to the point where he felt brave and invulnerable, a dangerous state, he ought to go home. But the thought of his bright clean kitchen with the floral wallpaper defeated him. He stayed.

"You don't find it depressing?" he said. "The dead Germans?"

"I'll tell you what's depressing," she said. "Creative writing is depressing. All these rich kids in the sandbox. I mean, the idea that you could get killed for saying something and then saying it anyway, the idea that any of this might matter, no—it's just *creative writing*, a something you can do for two years between college and marriage."

"I hope you're not waiting for me to disagree with you."

"I did think you might defend yourself."

"Not me," he said. "I'm just a visitor here. I don't believe I'm doing any particular harm but after that I'm agnostic."

"That's one way to live."

Winslow was in the presence of a romantic, he now understood: all or nothing, comrades to the barricades. Stuck in academic life and longing for the Revolution.

"It's not exactly like they would be out changing the world," he said. "If they weren't in graduate school they would be out making money like everybody else. Would that be better?"

"Agreed," she said.

"And at least they read," he said. "A little something. They keep the enterprise going. Nobody—nobody—buys books of poetry except the people who are trying to write it. At some point in the near future the whole thing will just collapse. Ten thousand typewriter makers and buggy-whip salesmen."

"There's a cheering thought."

"It was better to be Byron," Winslow said. "It was better to be a rock star. But I think those days are safely dead."

"That novel thing, that long poem—what would you call it? That thing you wrote about the girl, I loved that. In a better world, it would have made you famous."

Winslow felt his face flush red even in the cold, remembering that six-week fantasia where it *was* going to make him famous.

"Thank you," he said, stammering.

"That wasn't some little private moment," she said. "That was public, that was trying to talk to people, trying to say something. I loved it."

You and the starlet, Winslow thought. He didn't quite know what to say.

"Anyway, I'm glad you came," she said, and flicked her second cigarette out into the snow. Back to the fray. Winslow would have followed her but for his cigarette, still half smoked. And it wasn't clear she wanted to be followed—that little blurt about his book, the red-faced turn and flee. Maybe he would find her later. Maybe not. He had a glass of scotch in his hand and he drank it, looking at the snow drift down: individual snowflakes, the soft black of the sky. Snow reminded him of childhood, which made no sense as he had grown up in the rain. It snowed in Jewell once a year, twice at the most, and not at all some years. But even then, seeing snow was one of the few times Winslow remembered actually feeling like a child, feeling like he was having a childhood. Christmas, snow, a couple of camping trips and not much else.

Enough of that.

He went back into the party but Laurie was gone, apparently, or in some other room somewhere he didn't know about. Winslow refilled his glass with whiskey and surveyed the room: a hot loud box of chatter, sixty faces he didn't know and all of them laughing, talking, appearing to listen while scheming to talk. He thought if he could find Laurie Fletch's face he might look into one that recognized him, that said something to him, but she was not there. He wandered out of the kitchen and into the dining room, where the bones of a smoked turkey sat among decimated platters of cheese.

"I've been wanting to talk to you," said the man—a clean young man of thirty or so who dressed like his mother still dressed him, an earnest young man.

"You're the poet, right?" he said, pumping Winslow's hand. "I've heard about you from Maggie, Maggie Levine? My wife. She teaches in the department?"

"I've met her, yes," said Winslow, though he had no recollection of her at all.

"Stan Levine," the boy-man said. "She was telling me all about you. I can't wait to read your stuff."

"Well, thank you," Winslow said.

"I just saw you a minute ago and I just wanted to ask—these things, you ever have them looked at?"

He reached out to touch Winslow on the face: the temple, the ear, the forehead. He had soft hands, a soft touch, and although Winslow had no idea what he was up to he didn't really mind.

"The thing is, I'm a dermatologist," Stan Levine said. "I really think you ought to have those looked at."

"Those what?"

Levine led him to a gilt-framed mirror and pointed: a spot, another spot, discolored and rough.

"How long have you been seeing them?"

"I never noticed," Winslow said—and it was the truth, the sight of his own face in the mirror was nothing he looked forward to. Those corpulent lips.

"Come on down to the clinic on Monday and we can have a look," Levine said. "Come on down at four-thirty or so and we can sneak you in. You don't want to let those go without checking."

He grinned reassuringly, as if to say that this was all no big deal, but when Winslow said that he would come he took Winslow's hand and gripped it tightly.

"Good deal," he said. "I'll see you Monday."

Surrendering Winslow's hand, the doctor melted back into the throng, leaving Winslow to wonder what had just happened. The puppy! Winslow couldn't get his mind around the idea of a doctor twenty years younger than himself. Cops and doctors should always be older. And what exactly was wrong with his face? He turned back to the mirror and stared into its smoky depths, trying to see exactly what was wrong with himself.

And this was where Belva caught him again, staring at his own face in the mirror. "I know, I know," she said. "It's hard—hard to be as beautiful as you. Come have a drink with me."

Thus he found himself under the knife, under the big lights, in a clean gray room that smelled at first of alcohol. Levine was a talker, it turned out: about the weather, the skiing he had been doing, the music he had been seeing lately. He was a bluegrass fan.

This was unexpectedly fine with Winslow, who didn't mind talkers but normally wanted them to have something to say. But his forehead had been made completely numb with a shot of something—the prick of the needle and then the rush of nothing—and Levine was working up there as he talked, which meant that when he stopped talking Winslow could hear the sound of the scalpel. It seemed to be taking longer than he had thought and also to be harder work than he had expected. The smell of blood filled the little room, and then later, when they brought out the device to cauterize the wound—some kind of electrical skin-fryer—the smell of burning hair and skin.

"All done," Levine said cheerfully. "Nurse Betty here will give you the lowdown on how to take care of the wound and then we'll get the results back in a week or so."

He turned toward the sink to wash his hands and Nurse Betty—who was actually large and male and named Larry—came grinning into Winslow's field of view.

"You can get up now," Larry said.

Winslow was expecting what?—something different, more definitive. All the worry he had spent over the weekend and now this nothing.

"What's next?" he said.

Wiping his hands as if to clean himself of Winslow—the doctor had smelled the beer on his breath at this early hour of the afternoon, leaning into Winslow's face, and hadn't liked that idea at all—Levine said, "We'll just have to wait and see what the lab tells us."

"Tells us about what?" Winslow said.

"Oh," Levine said, "I hate to say the word *cancer.* It's one of those words that gets everybody all upset. But really, you know, it's a pretty good guess that they are, just from what I saw today."

"And what does that mean?"

"I don't know yet," Levine said. "Nothing, maybe. Probably. If they are what I think they are, we'll zip them out and that will be that. Time will tell. My advice would be to just go home and forget about it till we get the results."

"I will."

"You won't," Levine said. "I know it's hard but relax if you can. This will all most likely be fine."

Most likely be fine: the words repeated and re-formed, echoed and answered in Winslow's brain in the hours afterward. That fatal *most likely* was the worst, like the *do* when a woman says, I do love you. . . . Also the patented false cheer which the doctor acquired, along with his chinos and plaid shirt, at the mall somewhere. Bad, very bad.

The next afternoon Winslow sat with a jumbo mug of coffee and a whiskey hangover in his office, trying to make heads or tails out of the Second Elegy while the words whirled and twisted in his head. The new translation seemed as bad as the old translation but in a different way, and Rilke's words and Dr. Levine's words mixed and mingled. He had three different translations now—one he had borrowed from the library—all open on the desk in front of him, all the mighty, majestic German mixing with Levine's voice: If the dangerous archangel took one step now down toward us from behind the stars we'd just zip him out. It would most likely be OK if our heartbeats rising like thunder would kill us. And part of the problem was that in principle Winslow liked the doctor's voice better. He liked poetry that didn't sound too much like poetry, poems made with a carpenter's hand from ordinary materials, words you could find lying around, well-used words.

But the central part of the problem Winslow felt in his tiny airless office was the suspicion that there was something there for him. The Elegy was trying to tell him something and he was too dumb, too scattered and too drunk to hear it. He didn't know if this was right or wrong but he had a suspicion. That was all that Winslow ever had to go on: a suspicion, a faint smell in the air, a little something he didn't understand. Every time he was ready to write Rilke off as a ponce and a phony—roughly twenty times a page—he had to remember this suspicion, this little tickle in his nose. There was something there. What was it?

For as we feel, we evaporate, oh we breathe ourselves out and away. . . .

It seemed, at least, possible.

It was time to teach. He gathered his books and his coffee and thought—as he did each time on his way to class—that it might be easier if he just went out and got in his Lincoln and drove. He had no business here, not a thought in his head, nothing. The thought of those clean cheerful faces . . . And all the others, passing him by, would stare for a moment and then look away, frightened by the bandages on his face. Scared of the wounded one. The checkout clerk in the store the night before had looked at him with real fear, like he was going to rob her. Respectable people do not injure their faces.

"Bar fight?" asked Erika Jones.

"He came at me with a bottle," Winslow said. "I took him out with my bare hands."

Erika and the others waited for the real explanation but Winslow wasn't giving it to them. He sat at the head of the table and spread the different translations out in front of him and sipped his giant coffee. When he glanced up again, to survey the room, he found Erika's eyes on him and near tears from the look of her. He felt a shame that ran all through his body, down to his testicles. She was the one who was not meant to see his injured body. Ashamedly he turned away.

"All right," he said to the others. "Tell me what you believe in. What you navigate by."

A blank stare back at him, cows at a fence.

Winslow went to the chalkboard and drew a wavy line, a little boat with a little sail on top of the waves, a lighthouse on the far shore—a big tall stripy lighthouse with a nice big revolving mirror.

"Here we are in the nineteenth century," Winslow said. "It's a big confusing world but not too confusing—because if you get into trouble you've always got the lighthouse to steer by. God will tell you what to do. Sometimes he tells the King and sometimes he whispers it straight into your little heart, but you can't get into trouble if you do what God tells you. At least you can get out of trouble. Just steer for the lighthouse. OK?"

Annoyance, puzzlement.

Winslow erased the lighthouse.

"Now where do you go?" he asked. "What do you do?"

"That's the one that used to be in Portland, isn't it?" asked the tall boy, the one who made Winslow think the word *egret* every time he saw him.

"The what?"

"The mission," said the tall boy. "Down off of Burnside?"

"That's right, the Lighthouse mission. Same idea: God will tell you what to do."

Winslow turned to look at his own artwork for a moment and felt like the fool he was: a toy boat on a toy ocean. Too late to stop, though. He sat down at the table again and looked around at the expectant faces.

"Somewhere in here God stopped talking," Winslow said.

They knew this already, he could see it on their faces.

"It's an interesting question," he said. "Did He stop talking or did we just forget how to listen?"

It wasn't interesting to them. The impatience on their faces told him so.

"OK," he said. "Let's start over. Let's start where we started. How do you get through the world? With nothing, no light, no way to tell which way to shore or even to tell you whether it's better to be onshore or out there adrift somewhere. How do you do it?"

They looked at each other and then at him and apparently Winslow had started speaking in Egyptian again.

"You just do it," the tall one—her name was Penelope—said. "I mean, what?"

They laughed, which was within their rights, but Winslow felt a tiny spark of anger nevertheless.

"So nothing matters?" he said. "Nothing means anything?"

"It does to *you*," Penelope said—and from the looks on their faces, she was speaking for all of them. "You decide if it's something you want or something that feels right to you but nobody else can say that for you."

"No right? No wrong? No up? No down?"

"There is for *you*," Penelope said again, explaining it to the recalcitrant child. "It's like, yeah, that happened. I don't know. I don't really expect anybody to tell me what to do."

Winslow looked into her intelligent eyes and saw that she believed what she was telling him, that she had thought about it as much as she needed to think about it; then looked down at Rilke's angels, these silent emissaries from a silent God, resting there in triplicate on the page. Maybe it was true. Maybe Rilke needed to lighten up. Maybe Winslow needed to lighten up.

It was Dave—earnest red-headed Dave—who came to his rescue.

"You still need something," he said. "Even the idea that you don't need anything, that's an idea in itself."

Winslow looked at him approvingly, though he wasn't sure what Dave meant.

"What kind of an idea?"

"I don't know," the boy said. He gathered himself for another attempt while the others looked on and Winslow saw that they respected him, they were waiting for something interesting.

"I just think we value ourselves too highly," he finally said. "Our own abilities to see things, to know things. Anything we don't understand, that we can't put through the machine, make into a bunch of ones and zeros, anything beyond us, we pretend that it doesn't exist. Like where does the writing come from, for one thing. Something comes out well, I'm glad it came out of my mouth, you know. I think I wrote part of it but there's some part that I don't know where it comes from."

"The invisible," Erika Jones said sarcastically.

"I mean, is it any dumber to pretend it's an angel or God or a thousand-armed god than it is to pretend it doesn't exist?"

"*What* doesn't exist?" Penelope asked. "What?"

Erika Jones jumped in again, a little workshop animosity, good for the energy level.

"You can't put it into words," she said. "You can't just say it."

"Did I forget to smoke pot before class today?" Penelope said. "Did I forget to set my clock back to 1969? I mean, fine, there are things I don't understand, fine. I don't understand how an electric can opener works, much less the universe. But all this Zen bullshit about the invisible and the intangible, I don't know . . ."

"We're sort of stuck with it," Winslow said. Now, for a moment, he had their attention.

"Think about Cézanne," he said. "A bowl full of apples. Rilke spent a lot of time thinking about Cézanne to no apparent end, but whatever. So you see the visible thing, the bowl of apples on a table, right? What else?"

"You see how it felt," a blonde girl said: serious, clipped, one of the ones he hadn't identified yet. "You see what it looked like to the painter and not just, like, a photograph."

"OK," said Winslow. "What else?"

Silence: he had them stumped.

"What else?" he said softly.

At least they were thinking about it.

"There's a picture of some apples on a table," he said. "Right? And there's a picture of a mind and a heart and an eye looking at those apples and feeling them—even thinking about them a little. But there's something else, isn't there?"

A murmur of assent, a shrugging of agreement.

"What?"

He let the silence ring in the room for a minute before he went on, a sound he loved, a dozen minds in busy thinking.

"OK," he finally said. "But there's something else there, something that's not just the object and not just the perceiver and not just the relationship between the two. Some little whisper."

They didn't like this. Winslow didn't like it much himself but he was stuck with it.

"That's what Rilke is trying to catch in these elegies," he said. "That little whisper, that thing that's left over when you take all the things out of the poem that you can accurately name."

A further silent moment in which all of them—Winslow included—tried to figure out what he meant by this. Finally it was Erika Jones who broke the silence. She said, "Well, that seems difficult enough."

And at last they all had something they could understand and agree on.

Take a picture of Winslow that night, sitting whiskey-drunk in front of the television. He has never had a decent television before or cable either and now he knows why. There are three basic types of skin cancer and one of them, melanoma, is often fatal. He learned that in the library after class.

So here he is in front of the TV with a cigarette in one hand and a glass in the other and bandages all over his face. His face hurts but in a strangely disconnected way. Whiskey and pills combining, and Winslow thinks about all the newspaper stories of the drunk burned up in his own bed. I could do that, Winslow thinks. I could get there from here. He's watching a cooking show.

He's watching himself watch a cooking show.

Take a picture of him fat and drunk.

The Chinese boy in the screen is making something complicated. Winslow switches the channel and there is John Wayne and Donna Reed on an island somewhere in the Pacific. John Wayne is playing doomed and sensitive, the wounded skipper. I'd fuck Donna Reed, Winslow thinks, in a heartbeat. The story is a story is a story. The one thing Winslow finally understands is that it's only a story ever and what matters is Donna Reed, the speculation of those breasts beneath the plucky attitude and nurse's whites.

Which starts him thinking about his face, which sends him back to the Black & White for another round. He buys it for the Scotties on the bottle. He buys it so he can say *Scotties on the bottle*, if only in his mind. How about that? he asks the watching angel. How about them apples? The silent watcher from the other side of the Great Divide and all he's getting out of Winslow is little dogs and Donna Reed's tits. Winslow lights another Tareyton and wonders if he will live long enough to kill himself.

That angel, though. That watcher.

Winslow has an intuition, nothing more. Soon he will be on the other side to see for himself. The doctor's false cheer rings and reverberates in Winslow's head. Meaning? He drinks to the point of foolishness and beyond. If wishes were not horses. Take a picture of him here and now, the night that will not end, the morning that will never come, the blank piece of yellow legal paper at the end of the night. Take a picture of him.

"*I've never seen* a Cézanne," Erika Jones said.

Driving up to Hot Springs. Winslow was aware of her body curled into the passenger seat like a child's body, it took up so little of the enormous seat. It was easier to talk to her if he kept his eyes on the road but she was always there in the periphery of his vision. And this was easy driving, a cold afternoon and gray but not much traffic, no ice or snow, no danger. It took no more than half his attention.

"I don't think you're alone," Winslow said.

"No, I asked. Not everybody but a few people, and all of them had seen one someplace. Mostly in France."

"Go to France, then."

"Where's the nearest Cézanne to here?"

Winslow laughed. They were driving up the Jocko Valley— Winslow loved these names, Jocko, Arlee, Ninepipes—and the landscape consisted of barbed wire and cold horses and trailers and old machinery. Low mountains held the valley air, a gray sky low above. Gray or white or washed-out brown, even the cars were dirt-colored from the road gravel, and Cézanne seemed like another planet, another world.

"San Francisco, anyway," he said. "Maybe Seattle, I can't remember. Minneapolis or Chicago."

"Chicago is a two-day drive from here," she said.

Suddenly it was an idea between them: the two-day drive, the Art Institute. It had an instant plausibility—though instantly, too, Winslow knew it wouldn't happen. He could imagine it, though. He loved to drive.

"Have you ever been to Chicago?" he asked.

"Never."

"It's not much," he said. "I was there in the winter, maybe I didn't give it much of a chance."

"I love the idea of a city in winter," she said. "I used to read about them when I was little, Copenhagen and Stockholm. I was the only girl in Orange County who dreamt of going to Helsinki in January. Wasn't I special?"

"Where did that come from?"

"A fairy tale, I don't know. Some kind of children's book."

Winslow opened the glovebox and took out the flat pint of Johnnie Walker and handed it to her. She looked out the window: two in the afternoon, the flat gray light. Winslow watched her as she cracked the metal cap of the bottle and sipped at the whiskey inside. Winslow took the bottle from her and had a sip himself, no more than a sip. There was no telling where this afternoon might end up and so he meant to pace himself.

"I've never been to any of those places," he said. "I was in Paris once in February, though."

"And it was beautiful."

"It was all right," he said. "Everybody was dressed really nicely. I was there to see a woman who didn't want anything to do with me, which colored the experience."

"Did you know that when you went?"

"Did I know what?"

"That she didn't want to sleep with you."

"Oh, she didn't mind sleeping with me," Winslow said. "That wasn't the problem. She slept with me, she slept with her husband, she slept with her colleagues and her students. I mistook this for a genuine interest."

"Unlikely as that seems."

"Unlikely as it seems," he said. He noticed in a kind of abstract way that he was flirting with her, that he was advertising himself as a man of the world, one tiny step away from the brocade robe and the Hefner pipe. He wondered if he even wanted to sleep with her. He wondered what kind of bargain had been made when she offered to show him this place and he accepted. Her body in the seat next to his was so inconsequential and light—even in its layers of tattered sweaters—that he only thought of a child's body inside. This was what bothered him when he saw her in the corner of his sight, this child's body and this woman's voice coming out of her mouth. Better to keep his eyes ahead, fixed on the road.

Also there was this interference problem with the bandages on his face, like somebody tapping him on the shoulder every minute or so and interrupting whatever he was thinking about, this little hey, hey buddy.

Then he was remembering Paris, the city in winter, the well-dressed women in their long coats and boots, the sound of spoken French in the cold air.

He had met her the summer before, at a conference in Brittany to which he had apparently been invited by accident. Her name was Candace, some English joke for a last name, Winterbotham or Pinchbottle or something out of Trollope. She had the high fair good looks of a Trollope heroine, too, the tea-rose blush in her cheeks. Nobody knew what to do with him once he showed up, which was fine with Winslow. He stayed in his hotel room attempting to write until noon each day and then went for long walks on the beach, in the shadow of the old walled city. Later he learned that the walls were the same age he was; the city had been flattened by the Americans during the war and then rebuilt stone by stone, which gave a Disney air to the place, a familiar, reassuring atmosphere of fraud.

Still it was France and the food was good and Candace-with-the-English-name was his translator. This was his entire duty for this conference: one panel discussion about the future of poetry. Total blathering hell, as he knew it would be in advance, but cheap money for a trip to France. The discussion took place under a bank of television lights in a hall of six or seven hundred coffee-drinking French people around little tables, a few of whom were watching the panel, most of whom were watching a row of television sets down either side of the room on which the discussion was being played. It was the damnedest thing. Winslow asked but could never establish to his satisfaction whether this was being taped for future broadcast or whether this was all an elaborate charade.

The moderator of the panel, who apparently was an authentic TV personage, was tall and beautiful and long-winded. Either she had read everything in the world or she was adept at faking it. Three French writers, Winslow and a poet from Iceland—drunk as a dog at two in the afternoon—debated in French about whether poetry had a future, and if so, what? The Icelander paid no attention to the proceedings but once in a while would drop in a cryptic epigram, accompanied by much eye-rolling and loud laughter at his own joke.

The French debated vigorously while Candace—seated in the chair next to Winslow, leaning her head so close that he could smell nothing but her perfume under the hot lights—attempted to translate in real time: The English-speaking world . . . much slower in developing . . . a certain emphasis on the theoretical but they prefer to . . . something about the Wallace Stevens?

It was hopeless gibberish but mostly Winslow smiled and nodded and pretended to agree, which seemed to be what he was there for. Soon enough, though, it was Winslow's turn. The moderator turned her headlights on him and smiled and began to spit out a long sentence in rapid guttural French, a sentence that seemed from her expression to hold Winslow in some suspicion, a challenge perhaps. Winslow leaned his head closer to Candace's as the question entered its second paragraph.

"I can't understand her," Candace whispered urgently. "She's talking too fast."

Winslow, betrayed and angry, turned to look at her and Candace was flushed scarlet—the deepest, most profoundly sexual blush that Winslow has yet ever seen. And instant recognition of what it would be like to fuck her—that same sexual blush—was followed immediately by a desire to do exactly that. And maybe that would have been the answer that the French were looking for. Just take her down right there on the spot, under the lights, with a roomful of French to cheer them on.

It certainly would have been better than the nonsense Winslow did finally manage to spit out, some embarrassing hodgepodge of unfinished ideas and half-baked hunches. The only consolation Winslow could find was in the certainty that

Candace was no better at translating into French than she was in translating out of it. He saw this in the puzzled looks on the faces of the spectators, that fruitless groping, that Alice-in-Wonderland puzzlement.

And when she was done mangling his nonsense, his turn was over. The three wise men of France reassumed direction of the forum and Winslow joined the Icelander in eye-rolling and cryptic pronunciamentos for the rest of the hour. All the time, though, all the rest of the hour, he could feel the heat of Candace in the chair beside him, the hot blood coursing through her. It was like he already knew, like both of them already knew. Forty-five minutes after the panel was over they were in bed in her hotel room upstairs and an hour after that—after a brisk evening walk down the *plage*—they were in bed in Winslow's attic room overlooking the Atlantic. They couldn't keep their hands off each other. Looking back he wasn't sure if he even particularly liked her, a rich man's wife, nothing much to say—but just to say her name, just to think of her was enough to make him want her. Where was she now? What had finally happened to her?

Also this was adult adultery, an old-fashioned pleasure in a seaside town in France. He wore a tie and she wore perfume. They ate in town, in quiet and candlelight, away from the drafty tourist cafés in the old city with their endless platters of *fruits-de-mer*. They walked out to the old star-shaped fort in the bay and then sat on the parapet and watched as the tide rolled in and islanded the fort. And sex and sex and sex and sex. The heat she gave off constantly.

That was the problem, he realized, the difficulty with this girl sitting next to him: no heat. Light but no heat. He wondered what he was doing there.

Although when she suggested this trip, Winslow had instantly said yes. There were parts of him that were more straightforward. He wanted what he wanted. He wanted something to do with Erika Jones but it wasn't clear what.

The flat light of a winter afternoon. They drove across the Flathead River, which was the same color as the sky, half ice and half clear water, and Winslow wondered if there were fish in there. There had to be. He remembered in his body the casting motion, the moment of grace, the arc of the line coming off the tip of his rod and the quiet as it settled gently down onto the water. Winslow knew so little of grace that he held tight to whatever he could. He lifted his good right hand from the steering wheel and made the motion in the air, just to feel it.

"Are you conducting?" Erika asked.

"What?"

"This," she said, waving her hand in the air—and it did look a little like a conductor's baton, the way she did it.

"No, I'm doing something else."

"Oh, well, that's a good explanation."

"I'm glad you like it," Winslow said. "Are we there yet?"

"Almost. Another twenty minutes."

She sipped again at the pint of whiskey and handed it to Winslow, who sipped himself and wondered why it was a disappointment that they were so close to the end of the road. A tiny disappointment but still. It was the driving he liked, the beautiful in-between, neither here nor there, the sense of beginning. He was not sure even if he liked it here particularly—his eye had grown up on green landscapes, and everything here was cold and dry and grayish-brown—but the driving here was fine, a new little something around every corner: a horse, a tipi, a trailer half burned to the ground.

"Maybe we should," he said.

"What?"

"Just keep going," he said. "If we went to Chicago, I could show you a Vermeer *and* a Cézanne."

Again he heard the aging bachelor in his voice, the old creep. Have some sherry, darling.

"We could see the Corn Palace in Mitchell, South Dakota," he said.

"Is it worth seeing?"

"No."

"I have to be at work tomorrow anyway," she said. "Maybe another time you can educate me."

"I'm not trying to *educate* you," Winslow said. "I'll leave that to the English teachers."

"I just get tired of the rich kids," Erika said, shaking her head, earrings and nose-jewel shining. "You must get tired of them, too, been everywhere, got two of everything. Like they're always keeping score. Like I haven't been to Italy and that disqualifies me. I mean, fuck you. I've been to Poland."

Well, Winslow thought: hmmm. He sat back, wondering how he was to respond to this. Little Erika plainly had money, plainly had an impression of herself that was at odds with the truth. Mom and Dad's money, anyway—maybe they really were the ogres she made them out to be. It didn't seem like it to Winslow, though. Moments like this when she seemed about thirteen to him and he wondered what he was doing here at all and he remembered Levine's falsity, remembered that for all Winslow knew he might be dying. He tried to summon himself. He tried to find a suitably solemn point of view to face the coming difficulties from. But again he came up empty. In fact, he couldn't think of anyplace else he'd rather be than here, anything else he'd rather be doing than driving this empty windswept stretch of highway—a bowl of snow cupped between dry mountains and the road, a long curve down and in.

And how many men could say that? How many people in the world could truthfully claim that they wanted to be exactly where they were and nowhere else? Here, now, jingle-jangle thirteen-year-old girl and everything. Winslow found this thought cheering, and took a celebratory sip of Johnnie Walker.

This growing, mysterious sense of his own well-being . . .

They turned off the highway and down a side road and it felt to Winslow that they were moving backward in time with every mile marker. An old cement gym with a fresh coat of paint and the word GYMNASIUM in concrete above the door stood in its own weeds by the side of the road. Every car that came toward Winslow looked to him like it was leaving town for the last time and leaving a broken heart behind. Several boarded-up hotels stood overlooking the town, windows covered in plywood and the paint peeling off them and the big signs blank. The center of town was mud that smelled of sulfur.

It was like falling in love, the way he felt driving into town—that sense that this had been here all along, waiting for him, that sense of falling into place.

"The cowboys from out east, out on the plains," Erika said. "They used to come here in the winter. They had the hot baths and then they had the gambling, too. Terry was telling me, she's from here."

"That was a while ago," Winslow said, watching the empty storefronts pass by, the appliance repair shops and secondhand-clothing shops still hanging on by a thread. A bar at either end of the one live block: the Montana Bar at one end and Bar at the other, nothing else on the sign, just Bar. It was exactly like falling in love, not quite déjà vu but still the sense that this was here all along and waiting for him. . . .

"The reservation cops used to let them do anything they wanted," Erika said.

They parked in front of a big old hotel, a Moorish fantasy in the painted concrete of Winslow's childhood. Painted concrete in blue and pink, the Playland they used to visit at Seaside, the sound of skee-ball scoring bells. It was all there, all still happening somewhere inside. All it took was a simple thing to unlock it again: old concrete smoothed under generations of paint. Winslow found tears in his eyes.

Inside they paid an unwholesome-looking woman for the pool pass, she gave them towels and pointed them toward the separate changing rooms and again Winslow fell into his childhood: this time from the feel of cold cement floor under his bare feet. Standing naked in the empty echoing room, he became little Ricky, little Dick, little Dickeybird again, unloved, unlovable. He showered and changed into a bathing suit and saw himself in the mirror, which made him wonder what he was doing there: the grand piano of his belly and his small untrustworthy eyes.

"Don't get those in the pool," said the unwholesome-looking woman behind the counter.

"What?"

She touched the spots on her face where Winslow's bandages were on his, touched them lightly, like somebody making the sign of the cross.

Stigmata, Winslow thought, and blushed. He waved his hand to say that he would comply and went out into the cold afternoon in the bathrobe and trunks. The wind whistled between his bare legs, tickled the little fellows nesting inside. The pool itself was a painful fifty-foot walk across the driveway, under a crumbling portico. His bare feet recoiled at the gravel and ice and the whole project seemed unlikely and futile. Erika was nowhere to be seen.

But when he got to the pool, let himself in through the chain-link fence and disrobed and slid, inch by clumsy inch, into the hot water, his day became comprehensible. The water stank of sulfur and felt slippery against his skin, thicker and smoother than regular water, mineral and rank. At first he could not go any farther than waist-deep, standing in the shallows and basting himself with water from his cupped hands, but soon his body was used to it and he sank into the deep end, submerged himself to the neck. The water held him up. He sat on a bench feeling princely, kingly.

After another minute or two, just as he was starting to wonder where she was, Erika came out of the lobby. She looked uncertain of which way to go and wouldn't look at Winslow. It was shocking how thin her legs were out of the bottom of her t-shirt, how thin her arms were, how unsteadily she moved. Instead of coming straight to the pool she went to Winslow's car, and he saw that she was carrying a couple of little plastic cups. She had filled them from the bottle of Johnnie Walker and brought them each a drink.

When she got to the pool she set the cups on the coping and walked straight into the water and under, never looking at Winslow. He understood she didn't want to be looked at. When she came up again, only her head came out of the surface, and her t-shirt, which she still wore, flowed and fluttered in the water. The bright tattoo on the side of her neck continued through the wet fabric of the shirt.

"Cheers," she said, lifting one thin arm clear of the water, reaching for the cup, drinking.

"Cheers," he said.

But he had seen her, seen the thing he was not supposed to: the thin threads of her arms, the knees and elbows that stood out like knots in a heavy rope, the blue of her skin. Erika was not thin. Erika was dying, or something like it.

He smiled at her like an idiot but she saw through him, saw what he felt.

"Don't," she said.

And Winslow—with no rights in this matter, neither father nor brother—knew what she meant exactly, and didn't.

Did he sleep with her? He could not clearly remember the end of the night before. They had not slept in the same bed: Winslow could hear the girl breathing in the adjacent room of the tiny cabin. He remembered her telling him that she was a virgin and determined to die a virgin. He remembered the unwholesome woman chasing them out of the pool after they came back from the town bar and climbed the fence. All Erika's idea.

There was something else, though, not quite a memory.

Every day started out a little differently—a different set of plans and expectations, a different mood—but ended the same for Winslow, drunk and dirty. He sat up and bright stars flickered across his vision. His tongue felt like an insect leg in his mouth and the air in the cabin was stale with old smoke. Barely morning out, a dull light seeping through the curtains: seven-thirty. She would be asleep for hours if Winslow didn't wake her, and he wouldn't. He sat on the edge of the bed in his boxer shorts, sorry for himself and fat, unlovely. As in many other mornings, he had the feeling that he didn't fit his life, that there was some other life somewhere that he ought to be leading and not this one. This longing.

Also the usual dread that came with the morning after a drunk. Dread and regret.

He couldn't imagine it, somehow: his graceless bulk and clumsiness, her little breakable body. He wouldn't have even fit. Plus he still had his boxer shorts on.

Something more than usual, though—something in the end of the night before, some box he didn't want to open. This was a strange little cabin, he thought. Two tiny rooms with a bathroom in between, a faucet that ran all night, filling the place with the sulfur smell of the hot-spring water. Naughty pine, as a student of his had once written, and wagon wheels for chandeliers, pictures of the Old West. Was this what a rotogravure looked like? This would be a strange place indeed for anything to happen, small and smelly and unloved. Still he had the suspicion, the tickle in his nose that something had happened. What?

He got to his feet and he brushed his teeth and then took a long, satisfying piss. Winslow did live in his body. The large and small pleasures of the body. There was nothing ethereal about him.

He then pulled a t-shirt over himself and went to look at her, padding softly on bare feet. The little cabin was insufferably hot and stuffy with the afterlife of other guests but they had not noticed this the night before. A curtain over the one small window but the light came through it, faded as it was to near-transparency. The light was soft and gray and Winslow stopped cold when he saw her.

Erika lay naked with the sheets in a tangle around her legs.

What stopped Winslow was the way her pelvis looked, the basket of her bones showing clearly through the thin flesh. He nearly wept to look at her. The breasts, no more than a suggestion. The lines of her ribs. The tattoo was of a Celtic dragon and curled across one shoulder blade and up her neck. She also had a bracelet of thorns tattooed around one upper arm and a tribal design inside her ankle. People who thought they were going to live a long and happy time didn't get to look like this. The girlish tuft of pubic hair, soft and blond. *Pussy*, Winslow thought. A little shiver ran up his spine, a sense of trespass. Had they? She was naked, after all. And the deep certainty of his own guilt, without any particular knowledge of what he was guilty of. He tried to imagine, couldn't quite, how he could have done anything to her without breaking her. So small and slight and worrying.

Suddenly Winslow had the feeling that he was being watched. He looked around and there was no one, but still. Somebody was walking on his grave.

As quietly as he could he backed out of Erika's room without looking at her again. Somebody was watching, somebody was keeping score. He wanted to be elsewhere, someplace less guilty.

What was it about this place, though? Everything here exuded hurt and defeat, the brown knotty-pine paneling with decades of smoke on it, the sprung, exhausted chairs. He changed into his wet bathing suit and there was his childhood again in the cold clammy nylon. Without waking her or looking at her naked, he slipped out the door in his bathrobe and black street shoes, which made him look—he thought—like a character from an old stag movie: the naked white legs, the black socks and shoes.

A woman Winslow's size, enormous, was already in the water when he got there but she wouldn't look at him, wouldn't acknowledge his existence. Something was wrong with her: the way she held her head, something in her eyes he recognized from the day room in Salem. Some struggle inside her was lighting up her eyes. Nothing else in the hotel or the town was moving. Winslow floated in the slippery water, half perched on an underwater bench and almost asleep again, almost dreaming. *Descended into the older blood*, he thought, feeling the same outside and in, water and blood the same temperature and density and Winslow suspended between. . . . *Between*, he thought, always between—the child inside him and his own death approaching, if not in this disguise—and here he involuntarily touched the bandages, one, two, three—then in another and soon enough. The amniotic float. If we look back so fondly on what came before— and Winslow's earliest intuition of himself was a sensation of warmth, of floating, dust motes drifting through a ribbon of sunlight—then why is what comes after so frightening? Winslow felt like he could hold his whole existence in his hand or in his mouth, everything together.

He was going to have to quit fucking around with Erika, though.

At dinner the night before she had ordered a cheese sandwich and a salad. She then had eaten some of the salad, with the dressing on the side untouched, had cut the sandwich into pieces and moved the pieces around on her plate while keeping up a steady stream of bright articulate chatter meant to keep Winslow from noticing that she didn't eat a bite.

It wasn't vanity. It didn't feel like vanity, anyway. It felt like she was just indifferent. If there had been food she was hungry for, she would have eaten it. If she had wanted sex. It frightened Winslow, the way she was—nothing to hold her here on earth, nothing to keep her from spinning off. She liked to get high but that was not going to hold her. He wondered if she loved anybody, if she ever had. She would be a hard one to crack. She could love somebody and they might never know. She could easily do that.

The waters did their healing work. Winslow felt briefly like he was going to have a heart attack and die, and then he was better. The woman in the pool with him never once looked at him.

Winslow emerged from the water like a walrus flipping himself onto a rock. He robed and went into the lobby and bought the biggest cup of coffee they had and a pair of Danishes, wondering as he signed them to his room bill what the actual plural of *Danish* was. When he got back out to the pool, the enormous woman was gone and Erika was floating in her place.

"Danish?" Winslow asked.

"No thanks," she said. "I feel like shit."

Winslow searched for a nonsarcastic answer to this but there was none. For once he kept his mouth shut.

"I have to go pretty soon," she said. "I have homework."

He saw that she was unhappy—whether with him or with the weather or with the world, it was impossible to say. He was going to have to quit fucking around with Erika, he knew that again.

"We can get going anytime you want," he said.

"I'm not in any kind of hurry," she said. "I just have to get back."

Which half of herself did she agree with? But Winslow knew that she didn't have to make sense. She had feelings and they came out, came out in her words and on her face. Nobody had to make sense. When other people said you had to, it was just a way of making you speak their language. The world that wants you to do everything the way it wants. There was something wrong with her, something wrong with everybody. Maybe it was the place: the empty windows of the old hotels staring down from the hill. Maybe it was him.

"Let me finish my coffee," he said. "We can get going."

Erika lay back in the water with only her face out of the water and floated there with her eyes closed. Maybe she closed her eyes because she didn't want to look at Winslow, certainly not at Winslow eating a Danish. He sipped his coffee. He was all right with this. He was going to have to quit fucking around with Erika pretty soon anyway.

"Did I say anything last night?" she said.

"What kind of anything?" he said. "I don't know."

"I can't remember anything after eleven o'clock," she said. "I mean, I remember we were in the bar. I don't like that," she said. She opened her eyes and looked at Winslow.

"It scares me," she said.

"You ought to know better," he said. "You were having a good time, as near as I could tell."

"I just feel like I don't know how to stop."

"That's the problem," Winslow said. "I mean, historically, that's the problem. Once you get the ball rolling."

"You don't even worry about it."

Winslow found himself accused and as always he was guilty. But everybody makes their own deals. Let Erika Jones make hers, he thought. Let mine alone.

"At some point," he said in his most teacherly fatherly booming voice—attempting to shut her up—"at some point I decided that I was either going to have to stop drinking or stop feeling guilty about it. I didn't like feeling bad about myself all the time. It was impairing my self-esteem."

Erika heard the fraud in his voice and seemed to brighten. They were back to playing with each other, back to playing with words, never saying what they meant.

"Your self-esteem seems fine now," she said.

"I've recovered," he said. "Completely. Too completely."

She submerged herself and came up dripping with her hair slicked back like a seal. *Sleek*, he thought—and then remembered the injured body under her t-shirt, floating next to his. He felt both ways at once. Erika floated over next to him and then she touched his foot with her toe, skin on skin, soft underwater.

"Did we, uh . . . ?"

But Winslow was too preoccupied at first to understand her, feeling—even after she pulled it away—the touch of her skin on his own and wondering what she meant by it. Even without desire, and he didn't feel any desire for her, even without desire the easy intimacy of this felt right. It thrilled him, is what it did.

Only after a moment to feel this did he surface again to her question and realize this was what she was asking. A sudden flush of guilt, a knowledge deep in his chest that something was wrong with him, with both of them. Again he felt that echoing black confusion at the end of the night before, that thing, not quite a memory.

"No," he said. "We didn't. I don't think."

"You don't think?"

"I'm pretty sure."

"You're pretty sure? I mean, I don't know if it matters or not if neither of us remembers. The tree falling in the forest."

"With no one to hear," Winslow said. "Well . . . You were talking last night for a while in the bar. About how you were going to die a virgin."

"Oh, Jesus Christ," she said, and swam off, and submerged herself again. When she came up she would look only at the sky and not at Winslow for a moment. She was blushing and angry.

"In the bar," she said. "Fuck."

"Nobody was listening."

"You were."

"I thought it was interesting," he said.

"Of course you did. It's always interesting when somebody makes a fool out of themselves."

She shook her head, disgusted with herself, and swam under the water again to clear the dirt off her. Winslow knew the feeling: the dirt that wouldn't come off no matter what. The words which could not be unsaid. Really, he thought, she shouldn't be ashamed of herself. She was right, that if she wanted to be great, if she wanted to be a real poet, there were too many traps and snares in a woman's life. She just needed to learn to keep her trap shut. Nobody wanted to hear about greatness. But how many women had he slept with where they both felt something slipping away, and it turned out to be her? Stealing little pieces of her soul. And both of them wanting it because the other thing was loneliness.

"On the other hand," he said. "You might be wrong."

"About what?"

"Look at your boy Rilke," he said. "He was too good for life, you know? Too *sensitive*. Never settles down, has a million affairs but you know, you read his letters to his wife and it's all this high-minded crap. Total hell to be married to him except for all the interesting ideas. But it shows up in the work, it seems to me—he's so afraid of getting caught, of getting distracted from his big ideas, that it ends up feeling like he's afraid of life."

"Not to me," she said. "It doesn't feel like that to me. I mean, I'd settle down, find some nice husband and that would be it for me. That would be fucking *it*."

"Not necessarily," Winslow said. "I've seen it work."

"In *your* life?"

"OK," he said. "But it can work."

"Unless it's happened to you personally, I don't want to hear about it. Because the one thing I finally figured out is that you'll never ever understand what goes on between two people when they're in a *relationship*. Easier to see what's happening on the dark side of the moon. You can make up anything you want, looking at things from the outside, but the one thing you'll never be is right."

"We should go, maybe," Winslow said. He realized that he had been trying to talk her into something, trying to talk her into an appetite for life which she did not feel. And one of the few things Winslow had learned for certain was that you could not argue with the appetite. You could not talk people out of wanting what they wanted, or talk them into wanting what they did not want.

"I'm just relaxing," Erika Jones said. "I'm just starting to feel human again."

"I thought you had homework," Winslow said.

"Oh, fuck off," she said happily.

Sitting calmly in his office, reading bad student poetry, Winslow felt temporarily at peace with the world. A fluffy snow was falling out of a fluffy sky that afternoon, which seemed to have cheered everybody up. The students came stamping into the hallway with woolen scarves around their necks and snow in their hair and winter seemed plausible, even inviting, on a day like this.

Winslow himself had no driveways to shovel and no errands to run. He knew fairly exactly what he was going to say about the poems at hand and he was confident that the operation would go quickly and painlessly, perhaps even adjourning to the bar at the magical hour of six o'clock. It was a mystery the way this sense of well-being came and went but it was on him now.

Then Jack Walrath stuck his head in through the door.

"How's everything?" he asked. "How's it going? I haven't seen you."

"Everything's fine," Winslow said. "It's all fine."

Walrath looked at him doubtfully, came in uninvited, sat down in the guest chair.

"I haven't seen your wife at all," Walrath said. "We'll have to have you over."

"She's in Portland," Winslow said.

Walrath leaned toward him, expecting more, some whispered or murmured confidence, but there was nothing more to say about June Leaf. The name itself, just passing through his mind, sent off a reverberating pang of loneliness and loss.

"I've been enjoying the teaching," Winslow said, just because he had to say something.

"So I hear," Walrath said.

Nod nod wink wink.

Winslow felt the urge to pitch him out the window into the snow. Instead he said, "How is your semester so far?"

"Excellent," Walrath said. "We seem to have some really good students coming through the program. It really makes it easy."

"No doubt," Winslow said—and he did not doubt, because he had met these students, had moved among them, had heard from them in this office and in the bar after class how much they disliked Walrath. He would apparently have the students read the work aloud in class so that he would not have the trouble of reading it beforehand. He had not said an honest word—a real word, a felt word—to anyone in living memory.

"Hey," Walrath said, "I was sorry to hear about the thing, you know."

Winslow didn't have a clue what he was talking about until

Walrath—something contagious about this gesture—touched his own face at the places where Winslow's bandages were.

"Well, I'm optimistic," Winslow said. "We'll wait and see."

Walrath seemed surprised to hear him say this. He was on the point of saying something else himself but then changed his mind, shook his head.

"Oh, well, never mind," he said. "Glad to hear that things are going well! We'll have you out to the house!"

He fled Winslow's office in a flurry of exclamation marks—you could hear them in his voice—leaving Winslow wondering what had just almost been said. What did Walrath know that Winslow didn't? It couldn't possibly be good news.

His imaginary well-being had vanished entirely. The office shrank around him, leaving Winslow with an hour to kill before his class and nothing more to do with the poems in front of him. What did Walrath know?

He went for coffee, or something. Better still: he would go to the library, and see if they had a giant-sized reproduction of *Les Saltimbanques* for show-and-tell. They were at the Fifth Elegy already and the semester was racing past. Where had it gone? Winslow had been told that the library had exactly such a thing, and half an hour of blather over Picasso would shorten the class considerably. He had run out of things to say about Rilke, for the most part.

It had to be something the doctor knew, something the doctor told his wife, who told the department, who lived in the house that Jack built. Maybe the sky *was* falling. It was still snowing, anyway, big soft fat flakes that fluttered down like butterflies and made Winslow think of New England, though he had only been there twice, and never in winter. Inside the library was the hot close smell of winter, the heat up too high and the overheated young bodies in their wool and teddy-bear fur. A kind of flush that was almost like excitement, the snow outside and all of them locked in.

The prints room—yes, there was such a thing—was down two flights of stairs below ground level and down a corridor, so far off the main paths of the library that Winslow felt like he might get lost. But when he opened the door he ran into a familiar face.

"It's the visiting fireman," said Laurie Fletch. "The one-man rumor mill. How are you?"

She looked—as she had at the department party—thin, nervous and a little preoccupied, as if Winslow had just caught her at something. Still, he was obscurely glad to see her, shaking her bony little hand.

"What are you doing here?" she asked.

"I'm looking for *Les Saltimbanques*," he said. "The Picasso? I'm teaching Rilke, and all that's in the book is this awful tiny black-and-white."

"You're teaching Rilke?"

Winslow nodded.

"Get the fuck out of here," Laurie said. "I thought I was the only person around here crazy enough to try Rilke on the boys and girls. How's it going for you?"

"They like it better than I do," Winslow said.

"I believe you," Laurie said. "One hundred percent. I've been reading your work again and, man, if ever there was anybody who shouldn't be reading Rilke, you're it."

"Thank you," he said. "I guess. What are you doing here?"

"Oh," she said. "This is embarrassing. I'm on this self-improvement program? I figure if I can't get out to anyplace with real art I'm just, you know, my brains are going to run out of my ears. Cowboy art is not my favorite. So what I do is I check these out and I take them home and I hang them around my house for three weeks, until the library wants them back, and I pretend I've got a Chagall for three weeks, or a little Matisse. Just a little one. If I ever rob a bank, it's going to be because I want to buy a little tiny Matisse for my house."

"I think you're a little late," Winslow said—feeling a touch of contagious nervousness. Still, he liked the mobility of her face, her slender neck.

"I'm late for everything," she said. "Or early. I think I should have been born fifty years in the future."

"Why?"

"Because they would maybe have figured out what was wrong with me by then and how to cure it."

"You're all right," he said; which reminded her of something, she looked down at the floor again and when she returned to him her face was grave.

"Hey, I was sorry to hear about the thing, you know."

"I don't know."

"What?"

"I don't know anything about anything," he said.

"What do you mean?"

"You're the second person today," Winslow said. "You and Walrath both telling me how sorry you are but you won't tell me why."

"Oh, Jesus," Laurie said. "Oh shit. I'm sorry."

The student behind the counter glared at her, a Christian no doubt, an upright soul. Again a little spasm of terror reverberated through Winslow, and he made himself stand upright and clear-eyed when he asked her.

"What is it?"

"Oh, stupid me. It's gossip, it's nothing but hallway fucking gossip. I just heard that the tests came back not so good, you know, the . . ." And here she made the magic sign, touching the places on her own face where Winslow's bandages were.

"I see," he said.

"It's all secondhand," she said. "It's probably nothing."

"I'll have to look into it," he said. His voice sounded calm and even and strange to his ears, while the man inside was raging. That little puke of a doctor.

"I hope it's not bad news," she said.

"I'm sure everything will be fine," he said. And Laurie Fletch understood that he didn't want to talk about any of this—good girl, he thought, good Laurie—and began to edge away.

"I'm so sorry," she said.

"It's not your fault at all."

"I was going to invite you to dinner, too," she blurted. "This is not my decade to do anything right."

"I'd love to come to dinner," Winslow said.

She looked startled, then grateful. "Friday night?"

"My social calendar is blank," he said. "Friday night is fine."

"I'll leave directions in your mailbox," she said. "It isn't hard to find."

"Thanks for asking," Winslow said, watching her turn, watching her go. She left without her pictures. Winslow had apparently scared her off, which was only natural: people were afraid of the sick, people were afraid of the dying. Winslow let the word ring in his mind for a moment and wondered if it was only bravado, his lifelong gift for personal drama, or whether it was simple fact. Dying.

Dying: he turned the idea over in his mind as he paged through the racks of reproductions, each masterpiece done over in faded coarse colors like an elementary-school map and then encased in plastic—*The Polish Rider, The Night Watch, The Girl With a Pearl Earring, View of Delft, Sunflowers, Irises, The Artist's*

Bedroom at Arles. All this intelligence and fire all safely dead between layers of plastic. Hey, Winslow thought, these guys were all dead, Picasso, Vermeer, Charlie Parker. . . . With a kind of panic he realized that he had not yet done the work he was supposed to do and now it might be too late. The work that would outlast him had not been written yet. The body—which was never the best part of him—might be all that ever lived and died. Winslow was fucked.

He left the prints room empty-handed and walked preoccupied back toward his office, the light snow brushing his face. Two or three people said hello to him in the course of the walk but he did not look up to see who they were. In the office he took off his overcoat and brushed the snow from himself and stood for a moment with the lights off and the door closed, unwilling to make the call, resting in the calm gray light of afternoon, the long soft shadows.

When he called the clinic, after several layers of voice mail, the receptionist told him that Levine would not be in the office until Monday and could not be reached.

"This may be urgent," Winslow said.

"Who am I speaking to?" asked the receptionist in a voice that said that everybody's business was urgent and Winslow was no worse off than the rest of them. He told her and then listened to soft jazz in his earhole for a while. The little fuck. The little fuck was probably off skiing somewhere. Lying on the beach in Hawaii.

When the receptionist got back on the line her voice had changed. She said, "He didn't call you?"

"No."

"He was supposed to call before he left town," she said. "He wanted to talk to you personally. He didn't call you?"

"I promise you he didn't."

"Let's get you in on Monday, then. Let me look at the calendar. What time is good for you?"

This was beginning to feel like an elaborate sinister joke to Winslow. What time was good? No time was good for a business like this.

"Whenever," he said. "Anytime after, say, eleven."

"Eleven it is," the receptionist said. "We'll see you then."

The line went blank and Winslow sat down in his chair, again without turning the lights on, looking at his own hand in front of his face: soft, gray, almost transparent. He thought about the way he was still protecting his writing time: never making appointments for the morning, never taking a job that would interfere, always the best hours of the day went to his writing, even now, even when there was no writing.

Thursday afternoon: three days until Monday, four if you counted half of today and half of Monday. What was bad news? How bad was bad news? Winslow had gone to the library and looked up skin cancer after his first scare with Levine and already his life seemed small and fading away, like something you'd see from the windows of a passing train—the way he went to the library first at any event, any sign of trouble. Of course he was allegedly there to find out information, important and official. But the boy part of him, the part of Winslow he had always been, ran to the comforting presence of books, the place where he had a place, at any sign of trouble. And now it seemed like that boy might be going away, the careful plans, the discipline, the mornings spent on work that never was as good as he meant it to be; always a stepping stone on the way to the thing that he would eventually write, the part of him that would last.

It seemed like a bad idea to talk about Rilke that day. He went out into the hallway and found Dave, red-headed stalwart

Dave, and asked him to pass the word that he was canceling class.

"Is everything all right?" Dave asked. "Is anything the matter?"

"Everything is fucking ducky," Winslow said, and instantly regretted it. But to hell with the boy and his plainspoken face. To hell with all of them.

He went into his office and shut the door and assembled himself to leave: hat boots gloves scarf overcoat. He eyed the briefcase in the corner and thought about leaving it—he certainly wasn't going to get any work done—but then thought that he had better take it in case he never came back. He remembered that at one time, when he was in the Army, he had a list of things that he would do on the day he found out he was dying: he would start smoking again, he would ask Helen Rosenberg in the motor-pool office to fuck him. You wouldn't have to worry about the long run.

Eventually, of course, he had done all these last-minute things anyway: started smoking again, eaten like there was no such thing as cholesterol, drunk as much as his midnight self felt like drinking, asked Helen Rosenberg to go out with him, anyway, and it turned out she was married.

Walking down the snowy sidewalks, he thought that the one thing he had not counted on was the uncertainty. What the library had told him was that melanoma killed people but not everybody, not even half. It all depended on things he did not know—on the size and thickness of the tumor, on whether it had spread to the lymphatic system—and on luck. Maybe Levine was just scaring people. Maybe it was just a rumor. Maybe the Easter Bunny would come along and tell them all what to do. But Winslow saw it coming: indignity, fear, discomfort, prayer. And hope, the indignity of hope. He had seen it in the Army, he had seen it in Salem, every time Nelson Brightwater's daughters had visited: the blind, unreasoning hope that he would somehow be better this time, that their father would be ready to come home. No disappointment could dampen them, the fresh wound every time.

Home, the empty apartment. The light of four o'clock.

He turned the television on and then turned it off again. Plenty of time for the television. He sat at the kitchen table and tried to imagine himself reading. He opened and closed his refrigerator door.

In the end he went fishing again. The snow was continuing but the walk home had been fine, warm even in his coat. His things were in a duffel bag in the trunk of his car, no problem, and the river—a spot that someone in the department had given him, hidden inside the town, behind a junkyard—was only ten minutes away.

In his fingerless gloves and neoprene waders, he waded out into the clear water. Cars and trucks were passing by on the wet highway but Winslow was out of sight and unsuspected. The sound of tires on wet asphalt was the sound of Oregon to him. The water here was clear, the rocks on the bottom distinct, and between the falling snowflakes Winslow could see the rise-forms of feeding trout, rings on the water that moved with the water. Ungainly on land, sausaged into the rubber waders and dangling great quantities of crap, Winslow felt at home in the water. The river was wide and shallow here and the big trout were against an old bridge piling on the far bank. Slowly but steadily he made his way across the entire width of the river, through water that was almost to his waist at first and then no more than knee-deep. It was work, slogging even through the shallows, and he was sweating when he got there. Inside the waders he was fine, a little hot if anything, and the falling snowflakes tickled his ears. It seemed amusing to be out here in the snow, the snow accumulating on the banks but falling harmlessly into the water—a wet afternoon, the streetlights and headlights starting to come on.

Winslow lit a cigarette and watched the water until he saw the rise: a little sipping rise in slack water, with current between where he stood and the fish. A tricky cast and drift but the fish would spook if he moved any closer. Fucked if he did and fucked if he didn't but Winslow was something like happy, thinking about fish and not about the other. The other was there but nowhere near the front of his mind. He dipped the cigarette into the water to put it out and then put the wet butt into a film can which he carried in his vest for this purpose. The rise was tiny, which meant the bug was tiny, not that anything big would be out this time of day, this time of the year. Winslow noted again that the other thing was nowhere near him.

Far and fine, he thought, far and fine, tying a tiny Griffith's Gnat onto a microscopic tippet. The first cast, an experiment, fell two feet short of the fish, at the edge of the moving water. Winslow couldn't see the fly in the flat gray light but he could guess where it was. He let it ride along the seam. Just as he was about to rip his line off the water to make another cast he saw some subtle small movement in the water, behind where he thought his fly was but in the vicinity. When he lifted the rod tip, a small wiggling resistance came with it and then a small rainbow lifted angrily out of the water and shook his head at Winslow.

A small trout, yes: Winslow stripped him in without using the reel and got him off the hook with his forceps, without touching him or even taking a moment to admire him, as he usually did. The rough wool of his gloves would have stripped the fish of his protective slime, which Winslow thought he could use some of. Where is my protective slime? How thick was my tumor, he thought: a fine name for a very bad book.

A small fish, yes. But infinitely better than no fish at all. This trip was not wasted. He had been right to come.

Winslow cast again into the seam, and again, with no luck. He worked a little more line out and began to cast into the slack water behind. On the second cast into the pool, he saw his fly—he could actually see it in the calmer water—saw the fly drift down and saw a patch of the river bottom detach itself and become the body of a good fish and saw the good fish rise toward the fly at the exact moment that the current tugged at his belly-ing line and jerked the fly out of the fish's mouth. The dorsal fin and then the tail came out of the water and waved goodbye to Winslow as the fish left for Argentina.

Fuck! he shouted. It felt so good he said it again: Fuck!

Just the sound of the word coming out of his body felt good, the feel of it in his chest. Everything is written on the body. The body remembers: Reich's idea, that you carried the memory of an injury with you at the place where it happened. He used to run around punching people in the stomach and then curing them. That's what Winslow needed, some orgones, a little old-fashioned nutcase curation. And how much better was it to be wrong in an interesting way than it was to be right? Hurray for Wilhelm Reich, he thought, and fuck the FBI.

He cast till dark overtook him without ever seeing or even suspecting another fish, which was all right by Winslow. The important thing was getting out, and he was out. He smoked two more cigarettes in the stream, too, and these would be the best cigarettes that he would smoke all week. Best of all, he thought about rivers and fish and insects and not falling on his fat ass in the freezing water, and not at all of himself and his Problem, unknown as it was. He cast until darkness overtook him and then waded, cumbrous as ever, back to the bank where his car was, thinking the word *elephantine* over and over, letting the word ring in his head. The usual dire comedy at the car, trying to unlace his wader boots with fingers that wouldn't work anymore, snow everywhere and wet pants and darkness. Still, he made it, he didn't freeze, he lived through it.

The burning ache in his hands as the heater warmed them in the car, as they returned to life from numbness. Alive, he thought. I'm alive.

Erika Jones was waiting on the stairs of his apartment, waiting in the cold, the snow blowing around her. It was a surprise, a shock almost. Winslow remembered his trouble all at once. Her lips were blue with cold and she wore only a ratty overcoat and scarf, some castoff from the I-Love-Lucy rack at the Goodwill.

"How long have you been here?" Winslow asked.

"An hour," she said. "I heard, uh . . ."

"Everybody heard," he said. "Everybody but me. Are you coming in?"

"I thought you'd never ask," she said. "Do you have anything to drink?"

"I do," Winslow said, "I do"—his little heart performing circus tricks inside his chest. The thought of her out there in the cold and waiting for him.

"Excellent," Erika said. And followed him into the clean apartment, and turned to him, and touched his face with her cold, cold hand.

Laurie's house was small and snug and Craftsman-style with built-in shelves and fireplaces and brass lamps and furniture to match. As with Laurie there was something wrong with it, and as with Laurie it was hard to say exactly what. Everything matched a little too well. A fire burned in the fireplace and fresh flowers stood on the corner table when Winslow got there.

"Don't worry," Laurie said. "I don't have any particular designs on you. I just don't get a chance too often. I mean, buying flowers for yourself when you live alone, I don't know—it might be a sign of something. Can I get you a drink? I have nice wine, or vodka."

"Scotch?"

"Yikes," she said. "I should have figured that. I could look and see if there's anything in the back of the cabinet."

"Bourbon if you don't," he said. "Anything brown."

"Rum?"

"OK," he said. "Anything brown but rum."

He settled for vodka and they settled into the leather and oak of the living room. Laurie perched and hopped. On her third visit to the kitchen Winslow tried to follow her in, but she wouldn't let him.

"I mean," she said, "the whole reason you're *here* is so I can use my pots and pans and my living room. You know what it's like to live alone."

"It's been a while."

"Well, you're on your own now."

"That's not living, exactly. It's more like visiting. Waiting. It's like living in the waiting room except they are all my own magazines."

"Spring will come," she said. "You'll be back in Portland before you know it. In the bosom of your family."

"I don't have a family," he said. "I don't even have a bosom."

She looked at him quizzically—that little birdy tilt of the head. But there was no reason not to tell her.

"I think we're splitting," he said. "June and I."

"You think?"

"Well," he said. "I'm pretty sure."

"Jesus," she said. "You're having a fine month, aren't you? Between that and this"—and here she tapped her face—"it's just pouring down rain. What are you going to do?"

"I don't know," he said. "It's not so bad."

Laurie looked scandalized, and shooed him out of the kitchen. It did smell wonderful in there. When she came out again into the living room, she bore a little platter of mushroom caps, stuffed with something and then topped with something else and browned on top. She handed him a little plate, a maroon paper napkin and a glass of red wine, too. It was all a little complicated.

But the wine was good and the food was good and it was a cold night outside, with the wind blowing in the corners of the house. Laurie may have been unhappy but she wasn't particularly unhappy with *him*, except insofar as he was part of the male half of the race. Also, she had left three of Winslow's books—all the ones you could get hold of easily—out in plain sight on a table in the corner. She was making him welcome and it seemed like she was good at it.

"Where did you come from?" he asked her, when they were seated at the dining-room table. "How did you get here?"

"Oh," she said. "One second."

She rushed back to the kitchen to get something and Winslow contemplated his plate: a slab of salmon with suspiciously regular grill-stripes—a perfect X-pattern, in fact—and some kind of yellow sauce and a complex rice-based dish with things in it. A little fussy, a little complicated. She had brought him white wine this time.

"I forgot the garnish," she said, teaspooning some strange mixture on top of the rice: parsley and lemon something and garlic, from the smell of it.

"You like to cook," he said.

"I like to eat," she said. "In this town, it's simple self-defense."

He sampled the food on his plate and it was complicated and luxurious. Winslow, who normally liked uncomplicated things on his plate, had to surrender to her power here. He had to slow himself to keep from inhaling it all at once.

"You don't learn to cook like this unless you love it," he said. "Unless you have some gift for it. Don't you think?"

She sighed and sipped her wine and looked teacherly at him.

"It's a complicated little negotiation," she said. "I have a strange relationship with the domestic arts. See, I think men understand that—it's all performance to them, all for show. You know how many times I've been invited to a man's house and had him drag out the heavy artillery on me? I mean, pork roast cooked in milk, whole baby lamb."

"Really?"

"No, not really. But you know what I mean. But, like, nobody expects that that's how he lives, nobody's surprised when you go back on Monday and find him eating a microwave burrito in front of the football game. But, you know, you would come here tomorrow and find me in my sweat pants eating Top Ramen for dinner and you would think it was all fake, right? That I was trying to fool you into thinking I was a serious cook."

She looked at Winslow with a mixture of suspicion and expectation, but he couldn't begin to think of what to say.

Finally he said, "This is really good."

Laurie laughed.

"Not just more than you wanted to know," she said. "Ten times more than you wanted to know, and a theoretical framework besides. I'm out of my mind, it's true."

"I wouldn't worry about it," Winslow said. "Everybody's out of their minds anyway."

She put her fork aside again and once more Winslow saw the teacher emerge.

"It isn't true, you know," she said. "There are people with real problems."

"I know," Winslow said—and realized, as he spoke, that they both knew more than they wanted to say on this topic.

He said, "I just don't think there's anybody out there who's really seeing things as they are. I don't believe in the reliable narrator. You get deep enough into anybody's brain you're going to find a wiggle here and a wobble there."

"Somebody must be sane," she said.

"I doubt it," he said. "Not completely, not a hundred percent."

"Somebody must be happy."

"You think? I'd like to meet them," Winslow said, remembering—some faint echo of something, swimming into focus—Erika's comment about the dark side of the moon, the easy impossibility of knowing anybody. He thought of her with a small pang of regret and told himself that he was not betraying her by being here. Which he wasn't. He didn't want to sleep with Erika, and he didn't imagine that he would end up sleeping with Laurie, either.

Still some small sore point bothered him.

"Let's not get too cheerful," Laurie said. "We need to contain ourselves."

"No," he said, "I mean happy, like happy all the time. I don't think it would be possible, just based on the principle of contrast. If you want something to sound loud, you put it next to something quiet, you know, that little bit of red in a big field of white. You want to feel all of it, the whole range of things, to feel any of it all the way. There's a richness there."

Winslow shut up, embarrassed. He had been dispensing wisdom nuggets, which he had tried to swear off doing, except among the graduate students. Even Laurie, sharp-eyed Laurie, fell for it, though not for long.

"So you're saying . . ."

"Oh, never mind."

"No, it's interesting," she said. "It's all that cafeteria crap I eat at the university, all that Diet Pepsi I drink that makes the wine taste good. That certainly is a *useful* way to think. It gives a purpose to some otherwise pretty useless days."

"I aim to be useful," Winslow said.

"A purpose for suffering, even," she said. "That's pretty nifty. That is the quintessentially American way of looking at things, isn't it? I mean, Babel, you know, he was in Paris, he got his wife and daughter to Paris and then he *went back* to Moscow, a year before they picked him up. You know he lived for three years after they got him? I just found that out. He was in the same building for three years, KGB headquarters. Then they shot him in the head."

"Sounds pretty good to me," Winslow said. "Great way to live. What are you saying?"

"I don't know," she said. "I mean, you're right—it's nice in here, nice and warm, and you think about the snow outside and that just makes it better. A little bit of everything and then a little bit of its opposite, all nice and balanced and reasonable, I don't know."

Winslow had forgotten that he was in the presence of a romantic. Her apparent practicality, the cozy realism of her little house, had misled him.

"I didn't say *reasonable*," he said. "I never meant reasonable."

He sipped his wine and they both ate for a moment and Winslow thought of the blank face of the nothing that was approaching him, the mystery of the doctor's appointment on Monday morning, the empty space on his calendar after this semester was over. It even angered him a little. Here she was sitting in her beautiful house with her beautiful job and she was lecturing him on the uselessness of safety, the dramatic potential of self-destruction.

"I wonder if it isn't a mistake," he said, "to take rules of composition—which is all that contrast business is, of course—and apply them to life."

"Was I doing that? I'm sure I didn't mean to."

"No," he said. "I think I was. This dinner is wonderful, by the way."

"I'm glad you like it."

"You never told me how you got here."

She shrugged.

"Nothing special," she said. "I was an English major, I got a Ph.D., they offered me a job and I took it—and damn lucky to have it, too, three-quarters of the people I was in the program with are still waiting tables. A nice safe series of life choices, as I'm sure you noticed."

"I didn't say anything."

"I'm not trying to be great, though. I'm just trying to get by. That's what bothers me about all your boys and girls over there—they make these nice safe choices and then they expect them to pay off in the writing. They want to be great but they don't want to commit themselves."

Winslow thought she might be right but she plainly wanted to be argued with. And it was so pleasant being here that he knew he would try to please her in return.

"I don't know if that's what they want, exactly," he said. "I don't think they know what they want. They're all crazy, mostly."

"That one, Dave? He's in one of my classes. He's not crazy."

"No, he's not. He can write, too."

"You think he's going to make it?"

Winslow wanted to continue the argument but he couldn't—the gulf opening at his feet, the idea of what it might be like to succeed—which as near as Winslow could tell he had, he was as close to a success as there was, short of the two or three famous ones. And still he spent his mornings blank, staring at a sheet of paper.

"He'll do fine," he said, just because he had to say something, and began work on his food again, feeling his failure. The whole enterprise had failed. Cynicism didn't become him, he was better as a believer, but he couldn't seem to find a way out.

"What's the matter?" Laurie asked. "Worried?"

Winslow shrugged.

"When do you find out?"

"I go in Monday," he said "It'll be all right."

A deeply skeptical Laurie eyed him over the wreckage of the table. He would not be all right, it was true. But that was tomorrow, and this was tonight.

"Let's go smoke," she said.

"Go where?"

"Out on the porch," she said. "If you feel like it."

"This is your house, isn't it? Why do you make yourself go outside?"

"Oh," she said, "oh . . ."

And here she blushed a deep furious pink, shaking her head, sorry for the mess she had made of herself.

"Oh," she said, "I'm going to quit, you know? I'm always going to quit next week. And I don't want the house to smell like smoke when I do."

"I'm here to help," Winslow said. "Stay right there."

He went out into the kitchen—a catastrophe from top to bottom, every pot and pan and knife and bowl was dirty on the counter—and found a suitable small plate that said *Indiana State Fair* on it and had a picture of a cow and a sheep and an ear of corn below that. He brought it back into the dining room and set it at her elbow and said, "This will work."

"I have ashtrays," she said. "This is not an ashtray problem."

"It's a psychological problem," he said. "I know. I'm here to help."

She looked up from where she sat, and Winslow saw disappointment in her eyes: he was pushing her around, he was like the others, she'd thought he wouldn't be.

"There's eight inches of snow out there," he said. "You'll catch pneumonia one of these days. Either that or we can go to my place."

Her eyes were still doubtful.

"How many luxuries are there?" he asked. "How many advantages to living alone? We can at least give ourselves this."

Slowly and still doubtfully she got up, reached on the mantel for the pack of cigarettes there and the purple Bic lighter and then found a real ashtray—in hammered copper, a real grandmotherly souvenir—in the shelves next to the fireplace. She changed her mind a half-dozen times but finally sat down again and lit a cigarette and slowly exhaled into the still-warm air. Then turned to Winslow.

"You are the devil," she said.

"I try."

He lit a cigarette himself and sipped his wine and luxuriated, watching Laurie slowly unbend to the pleasure of the evening.

"Speaking of which," she said.

"What?"

"Are you sleeping with Erika Jones?"

Winslow's pleasant mood evaporated in an instant. He had to control himself carefully when he said, "No. Am I supposed to be?"

"According to rumor," Laurie said. "What is a scuttlebutt, anyway?"

"I have no idea," Winslow said, and this time he couldn't

134   *Kevin Canty*

keep the anger out of his voice. Laurie heard it and looked into his face, surprised. The entire playful evening gone in an instant.

"I'm not sleeping with her," Winslow said.

Not that it's any of your business. They both heard it, even though he didn't say it.

"I'm not accusing you of anything," she said. "Erika's an interesting girl. There's something missing in her, something that draws people in, don't you think?"

But Winslow didn't want to change the subject, not yet.

"Why does anybody care one way or the other?" he asked. "Why is this anybody's business but mine?"

Her mouth pursed again into a teacherly set line and she developed her line of reasoning.

"The good old days," she said. "The good old days where the girl poets were one of the fringe benefits for the professors, those were not good days for the girl poets. They thought it would get them taken seriously by the class or by the professor. They thought they would get to be mistaken for adults."

"OK," he said. "Unsightly business all around. But was anybody really hurt by it?"

"I was," Laurie said. "I don't know about anybody else."

Winslow stubbed his cigarette out and sipped his wine and only then did he look into Laurie's face, which was searching his, searching for signs of guilt.

"I'm sorry," he said. "Sorry you ran into a bastard."

"He wasn't," she said. "He was a perfectly nice person who was well within his rights according to the rules of the time. But the rules are different now."

"I'm still not sleeping with Erika Jones."

"I know," she said. "I'm glad you're not. She's just somebody we all try to protect, I think. We're all scared for her."

"You should be," Winslow said.

"When she was in the hospital last year, it was like a branch of the department in there. Everybody visiting and flowers and all."

"What was she in the hospital for?"

"You know," Laurie said. "That silly girl disease she's got."

"What happened?"

"I guess her liver started to shut down," Laurie said. "That's what got her into St. Vincent's in the first place. Then they had her on the psych floor for a while. She didn't tell you?"

"I didn't ask," he said.

"What do you two talk about when you're out driving around?"

"Poetry," he said. "Among other things."

Laurie's skeptical face on his. But it was almost the truth.

"You ought to talk to her," Laurie said. "She's killing herself. What she does is she gets to be your friend, she was my friend for a while, she was Belva's—then, when you bring it up with her, she goes out and finds a new friend that won't get in her face about it. You'll see."

Winslow didn't like her telling him what to do but he felt how she felt it—the jilted friend, the left-behind—and felt, too, his own sorrow and helplessness at the sight of Erika's body, the disfigured thing. The left-behind.

"I don't know," he said. "I'll see what I can do."

Dessert and coffee: a grown-up evening. They were back talking easily again but the memory of Erika persisted. Laurie left the kitchen a mess, shutting off the light so she wouldn't have to look at it, and brought her cigarette and a bottle of cognac and two small bulbed glasses out to where Winslow sat in the living room looking through an enormous picture book by Garry

Winogrand. He had heard the name before but this was something: three hundred pages of pictures of nothing, and every one of them terrific.

She put the glasses down on the coffee table and found a CD after a minute's fuss: Dave Brubeck, of course it would be Dave Brubeck. Winslow felt like he had time-traveled back to his own college days. Then realized that she had put it on—no doubt—in tribute to him. If Winslow were not there she would be doing the dishes and listening to Led Zeppelin or something.

She poured them each a healthy dose of cognac—good girl, Laurie!—and settled into the couch next to him, more closely than he was expecting, looking over his shoulder at a photograph of a laughing girl holding an ice-cream cone. "Isn't he terrific?" she said. "It's right there in front of your eyes but he sees it, somehow, and I never do."

"I never see what's in front of me," Winslow said. "I never know till later. That's why I write, I think—to find out what actually happened to me. To remember and try to understand."

"Do you?"

"Sometimes I understand it better," he said. "Sometimes it feels just as impossible as ever. Anything from childhood, you know."

"You never had children yourself."

"No," he said.

"I wonder," she said. "The way the grown-ups loomed in life, like gods, you know—big powerful distant gods. I wonder what it would feel like to be that person. Probably nothing like it felt from the other side, you wouldn't even know it was happening."

"You never had children?"

"Not me. I've been busy."

"Have you ever been married?"

"Three times," she said. "Between me and my sister in Florida we've been married seven times! Apparently we like to get married."

"Apparently."

"But we don't have a knack for staying married. You should see the pictures from her last wedding. Everybody stays friends, that's the problem—all her ex-husbands and their new wives, everybody showed up. She's got kids, too, one from Tony and one from John. It's quite a mess."

Sitting, talking with Laurie in her warm living room, a full stomach and a pleasant—though not incapacitating—buzz from the wine and cognac, Winslow realized that he was having a large and mistaken feeling, in which he was the father and Laurie was the mother and Erika their little child; some improvised warm feeling of family, of belonging, of everybody in their place and liking it in their place. And although he knew this feeling was wrong, this didn't stop him from feeling it, or from enjoying the feeling. If temporary and mistaken comfort were all he could find, so be it. The feeling of belonging here, the feeling of fitting in, the quiet light and dim music.

So it really came as no surprise to him when he turned his face away from the book of photographs and there was Laurie, ready to be kissed. Certain aspects of the evening suddenly fell into place, things that had been puzzling him: the books on the table, the flowers, Dave Brubeck. He would be a bad sport to refuse her and he did not.

She looked up again after the first kiss, a soft, thinking, tentative kiss.

"I don't mean anything by it," she said. "I'm not serious."

"No."

"We can keep our clothes on," she said.

"That's fine."

"I just have to make sure everything's still working once in a while."

"Be quiet," he said, and she was. Another kiss, and another— an old-fashioned slow-paced evening of necking on the couch, and only a few minutes into it did Winslow realize how much he wanted this. Slow, decorous necking, stopping for drinks, lighting cigarettes and touching hands. He touched her breasts through the fabric of her dress and her bare legs under but he knew they were going nowhere, which was fine; just the night, and the warmth inside, and the touch of her pliable scented skin, the hot blood under the skin. And it was not until she stopped and excused herself to go to the bathroom—and even this was welcome, a kind of welcome intimacy—that Winslow remembered Erika waiting for him on the steps of his apartment, waiting in her old coat and her ratty gloves and blue lips. And even when Laurie came back—when she poured them each another shot of cognac and they resumed their aimless, heartless kissing—even then he could not forget her, a little blue-lipped face, a little cold spot in his heart.

Winslow was afloat in his inadequate tub when he heard his doorbell ring. He thought briefly of getting up and answering and then thought better of it. He knew who it was, and if it was not her, he did not want to see them. And if it was Erika, a closed door wouldn't stop her.

"Hey," she said through the door.

"Hey," he said.

"Can I come in?"

Winslow thought about it for a moment; he did not want to be seen, was the problem—did not want to be in his body, the guilty, injured thing.

"You'd better not," he said.

"All right," she said. "I've got whiskey, though. How did it go today?"

"I'm all right," he said.

"What does that mean?"

"I'm going to live," Winslow said. "He said he was almost sure. He said it was a nice thin tumor that didn't get down into the subcutaneous part and with a little radiation I would be just fine, probably."

"Jesus Christ."

"I know," he said. "One second."

He rearranged a washcloth to cover himself, his limp one-eyed blind fish, and said, "You might as well come in."

He lay back against the porcelain with his eyes closed, so he wouldn't have to look at her face once she saw him.

"Oh, Jesus Christ," she said. "Oh, Richard. What did they do to you?"

He shook his head, his eyes still closed. Then felt her approach, reach down, felt her cradle his head in her small hand and reach down and kiss the smooth uninjured dome of his forehead. He didn't open his eyes again until he felt her move away.

She was still staring at the bandages, one of them blood-stained, the black eye he had sustained in the battle.

"I'm sorry," she said, and looked away.

"No, that's fine. I know I'm quite a sight."

"Radiation?"

"Starting next week. I'll be all aglow."

Erika slumped down on the linoleum floor, her back to the wall, and brought a bottle of Johnnie Walker from the pocket of her ratty overcoat. Winslow already had a glass of melted whiskey-flavored ice next to him on the soap rack. She filled his glass first and then drank from the bottle herself.

"Thank you," Winslow said, turning the hot-water tap with his foot and filling the tub a little higher.

"How did this happen?" she asked. "Did they say?"

"The only cure is the time machine, the doctor said. He told me if I could go back to when I was eighteen and quit getting sunburned all the time . . . All this happened years ago."

"Helpful," she said.

"Well," he said. "If I was feeling even more like an asshole than I already am, I would point out that it never occurred to me that I ought to take care of myself when I was younger because I never thought I would get old."

"And now you're old," she said, "and you're still not taking care of yourself. Fuck you."

"Sorry."

"It's all right," she said. "This light is killing me. Mind if I do something about it?"

"Not at all. Bring me a cigarette, would you? They're on the coffee table."

She came back with an ashtray, a pack of cigarettes, a lighter and a candle, turning the light off on the way into the bathroom. In the sudden dark he could feel the weight of a winter night pressing down outside, and the flimsy provisional warmth of this apartment.

"What are you doing with an artistic candle, anyway?" she asked. "This thing has got, like, *leaves* pressed into the side of it."

"It was here when I got here," he said. "I think it's part of the decor."

"What?"

"Never mind," he said. "Go ahead and light the fucking thing. The university isn't paying me all that much—they can afford to throw in a candle."

She lit it, lit a cigarette for each of them, and as she passed his to Winslow he saw her grimace when she raised her arm.

"What's the matter?" he asked.

"Oh, shit," she said.

"What?"

"Nothing."

"What kind of nothing?"

"Oh, Richard," she said. "I fell down the stairs at Dave's apartment last night."

"How did you do that?"

"I was drunk."

She said it lightly, as if it was a joke—a joke he was in on, something Winslow would understand—but he heard it differently. It was like a door opening in front of him, a stairway going down. Again, she was not going to live. She was not going to be all right.

"What's wrong with your arm?"

"It's my shoulder," she said. "Nothing's broken. The good news is—you remember that pain in my side?—it's gone now. I must have knocked it back into place, whatever it was."

"There's a bit of good news," he said.

"That's me," Erika said. "Always on the sunny side."

She leaned back against the wall again and Winslow saw, again, that slight wince as her shoulder touched. He lay back smoking, regal, watching the flickering shadows from the candle-flame across his bathroom ceiling. This very temporary comfort, safety, warmth.

"What are you going to do?" she asked.

"About what?"

"After this semester," she said. "What are you going to do then? Are you going back to Portland?"

"I don't know," he said—and realized, as he thought of how to answer this, that he wasn't anxious to talk about June Leaf with Erika. Unfinished business there, unless it was finished, which it might be. He was saving much of the money he was making, he would end up with enough to get by for a while, someplace, doing something. Waiting for nothing.

"You don't like it here?" she said.

"I'm starting to. I haven't been through a real winter in a while, it's kind of interesting."

"You like the *winter*?"

"I like things I can touch," he said. "Nothing too subtle. Nice and gray and depressing, plus you get car crashes and snowstorms, nothing wrong with that."

"You're fucking crazy," Erika said.

"Thank you," he said.

"Look, let's just go," she said. "You've got a nice big car. Let's get out of here, go to Mexico or someplace. This is just suffering. That's all you're doing here is suffering, and it can't be good for you."

She felt sorry for him. All this time he had mistaken it for something else but really she felt sorry for him and kept him company to keep him from feeling lonely.

"I have to stay," he said. "I have to teach. Also, I have to get myself radiated."

"You could do that anywhere," she said. "And you don't need the teaching. I mean, maybe you get something out of it that I'm not seeing but I don't know what that would be."

"I need the money," Winslow said.

"You're not doing this for the money," Erika said.

"Oh, but I am," he said. "I don't have any money."

And he realized as he said it that she did have money, that she always had money and always would—or at least had been brought up to believe in money without end. The ratty sweaters and one-room apartment were questions of style, unearned. This was nothing he wanted to know about her. Erika was shrinking on him. She wanted to get in the car and drive, just like Jack Kerouac, just like the silly pop songs on the radio all day.

"Here in the real world," Winslow said, "people have to

work for money. I do, anyway. Maybe you should join the Army for a while."

Out of the corner of his eye—he was staring at the flickering shadows on the ceiling—he saw her wince again, the same quick pain, except that this time it was Winslow that did it.

"Thanks for the advice, Dad," she said.

"Sorry," he said. But he was still angry with her, her little rich-girl mannerisms, her rich-girl disease. Nobody would call her on it.

"Look," he said. "I don't have a choice, I have to live in this world. There's nobody to take care of me."

"Nobody's taking care of me."

"I know," he said. "That's why I'm angry with you."

She stubbed her cigarette out curtly and Winslow knew that he should stop talking—knew that he should have already stopped talking. But it was too late for that.

"I'm getting out of the tub now," he said.

Erika didn't move.

"Please," he said.

"Are you afraid I'll see your dick?"

"Please," he said again. "I'll be out in one minute."

She got up then and left him, turning the big light on as she left. It came on bright and hard and Winslow knew then that he had made a mistake. This was not the night for big questions or hard conversations. Really, they had been fine until he screwed it up. A little peace and quiet, a little conversation, a few drinks and an early bedtime. What was he thinking?

But it was too late now. Erika sat at the kitchen table curled into an angry little ball as he made his way from bathroom to bedroom, feeling vaguely regal, vaguely Roman with his towel draped around his waist. Damp and tired and wrung out. He dressed in his usual, his always clothes—white shirt, chinos, black socks and shoes—his uniform, if it came to that, a way of not thinking about clothes, which was best. He put his decent wristwatch on again and remembered the feel of the knife on him, the dermatologist rooting deeper into his face, the smell of blood and the feeling of injury. Violence had been done to him, even if it was healing violence. What would she know, this little girl.

And why couldn't he go back to fifteen minutes ago and shut himself up?

He felt like his blood was angry inside him, he felt like his blood wanted to come out of his body again. One wrong move and the stitches would open up again and the blood would come pouring out, all of Winslow inside-out on the floor. Really, she should go. He was no kind of company.

"You're going to tell me how to live?" she asked, when he sat down across the table from her. "You're going to tell me what to do? I'm looking forward to it."

"I think you should go," he said. "I'm no good for company tonight."

"I thought you had something to say."

"I'm just angry with you," he said, as softly as he could. "The same as everybody else."

She looked up, disappointed and angry. He was just like all the others. He was no better than any of the rest of them. Winslow tried to find within himself the ability to take it back, to forget—for this evening, anyway—that she was killing herself, taking herself away. But this was not all right with him. It was not going to be.

"I have my problems," he said. "I'm not perfect, I know that. And it's none of my business."

"Now what could possibly come after that?" she said. "What could you be getting ready to say?"

"OK," he said. "I won't say anything."

"Thank you," she said. "Fuck! Why does everybody want to talk about my *problem*? You don't have a *problem*? Nobody else has got a problem. That's why everybody's so fascinated with mine."

"You're going to die if you keep this up," Winslow said. "I don't want you to die. I would miss you if you were dead. It's not a lot more complicated than that."

"Well," she said, "practice up."

She took her whiskey bottle and her ratty coat and she was gone, a blast of cold air from the open door all that was left behind her, a smell of paraffin in the air from the ugly, stupid candle she had blown out. Winslow sat down at the kitchen table, across from the blank place where she had been. He sat as if he was about to start explaining to the empty chair. He had more to say and no one to say it to. After a moment he got up to fetch his glass of melted ice from the soap shelf next to the bathtub. How quickly things change. The peace and company he remembered here were only minutes away but gone, maybe gone for good. Why couldn't he have been born with the wit to keep his mouth shut?

But he said what he felt. When he knew what he felt, he said it out loud, which was the only way he knew to live. Otherwise nothing ever got on the table, it was all just buried intentions and bad feelings.

With no rights in this matter, neither father nor lover . . .

He sat down in front of the television and lit a cigarette but neither had anything for him. The smoke tasted hot and sharp and bitter and the television was just noise and color, noise and color punctuated by bursts of false applause. He shut the box off and went to the window and she was really gone. The cul-de-sac parking lot was deserted and dark and cold-looking, as if none of the cars had moved for years. But she had been there only a moment ago. She had been here, with him.

Winslow was alone.

Winslow was old and injured and tired and he was going to die alone. Nobody loved him; or if they did, they couldn't live with him. This was a bad night, no doubt. It was still only eight o'clock. The cold wind blew snow horizontally across the asphalt and nobody came by. The futility of it. He had to start again and he didn't have the energy to start again or even the time. He wasn't twenty. He wasn't going to develop a new career, a new approach, a new way of looking at things, a new anything. Sick of himself, stuck with himself.

He felt tired and restless, all at once. He wished that she was back with him. He should not have driven her away.

But she was barely twenty, nobody for Winslow. He was only using her as a way of not thinking about his difficulties. When she was with him, he could ignore the blank place looming after the end of this semester, the mystery of his life. He found himself wanting to explain this to her, wishing Erika was here so he could tell her why she shouldn't be.

This was certainly pointless enough.

He went back to his couch and his TV but something had happened to him. His immunity had worn off. He was dying, he had always known that much—everybody was dying from square one, quickly or slowly, some people knew it, some people didn't, some people brought it on, encouraged death, embraced it, while others fought—but tonight it felt different. Tonight he understood that this was going to happen to him personally. Whatever he felt, whatever he did, whatever he thought about it, Winslow was going to die.

Not from this silly cancer, he understood that. Not from

love and not from loneliness. He was going to die from some other silly cancer or accident, some regular workingman's death. He remembered that moment in Hawaii, turning the wheel of the army-soldier-green Impala into the tunnel abutment: how light it was, how small a movement. Really it was almost nothing, an inch. But that was something else, some other, braver version of himself that had taken that particular plunge. Now he had lived life long enough to become attached to it. If he did not love life, he was at least used to it, and quite unready for a change.

But everything that belonged to Winslow was going to be taken from him. Today, tomorrow, next week, next year. Bits and pieces of his world were already gone, and giant pieces, too: his mother, his father, the uncles in their red suspenders who smelled of wet wool and sawdust. The wino bars of downtown Portland were long gone, and the afternoons of the poor clean retired ladies in the old apartment buildings in Northwest. These things had once belonged to Winslow and they were gone. General MacArthur versus the Japs. The bad Russians. Once they were omnipotent and nuclear and evil and now they were a bunch of jokers who couldn't drive a tractor. It was a smaller world, and shrinking.

Maybe that was it, he thought: maybe you just got to a point where everything around you was strange, where the world had changed sufficiently that you no longer fit in it. None of the music sounded like music anymore. None of the dancing looked like dancing. The satin-and-powder fancy world that he saw in the movies—where was it? He had grown up expecting to inhabit that world, and now even the memory, the fancy of that world was disappearing from the earth and he had still not slept with Carole Lombard or Barbara Stanwyck.

Even his suffering was ridiculous, he understood that, too. His fucked-up face.

All of it taken from him. That was what he felt: all that he knew and all that he loved was to be taken from him, and soon.

He understood that this was what he had been waiting for. Another little lollipop for Winslow the ever-intelligent boy: he had solved the mystery, he had decoded himself. But really it felt like he had touched some sort of rock. Perhaps he had at long last found a bottom, a solid place to start. A place to turn, a way to go from here. He thought of Erika's tiny angry face as she was going, gone.

What was left: the one thing he'd always had, the center, the blank piece of paper, the place he could always go. Look at Winslow on this cold night, still damp from his bath, still bleeding from under the big bandage, injured, tired, slow. In doubt and in exhaustion he pours a fresh slug of scotch and sits down at the table with a pad and pen—an ordinary ballpoint, anything fancier would ruin his luck. He writes the first words on the page: HOT SPRINGS. Then lights a cigarette and regards his own writing, an antique hand, sprawling and messy but with the old flourishes of the Palmer Method intact. The words seem small and futile on the page, as ever. Then adds the words below, in smaller letters: *for Erika.* It's a start, anyway. He can imagine something happening next. He can't imagine what. He smokes his cigarette and sips his drink and regards the words on the page, waiting for the reaction, the next thing, then thinks: You might come here bleeding. Then writes these words on the page and waits for the next thing to come, knowing it will—whatever the thing wants to be, whatever the shape is, already out there in the ether somewhere, waiting for Winslow to discover it, to translate it into words and then copy the words onto a page. And then immediately the second thing starts to take shape, a letter, *Dear*

Erika, it will start, *I have been meaning to tell you . . .* and immediately the third comes to him, carrying the featherweight body of Mrs. Esterhazy down the stairway when she broke her hip—the first painful step in her own death, she lost control of her bowels and smelled of shit and she knew Winslow could smell it and seemed almost more concerned by this than by the fact that her body was once and finally broken.

OK, he thought. All right. The mania was back. He knew it all and was ready to say it. Ten feet tall and bulletproof. But this was his, as much as he had, and it was back, and Winslow—for now—was Number One with a bullet. Winslow was back.

Even Rilke was easy. The next morning, before class, he reread the Eighth Elegy and for the first time Winslow felt like he knew the man, like he could stand chum to chum and talk poetry business with him, the way he once imagined himself in conversation with Auden and Eliot and Yeats. Shoulder to shoulder they were moving the enormous wheel of poetry forward.

Limpid was the word on the page before him. The poet's intentions and his methods were clear to Winslow, as was the light behind, the moment of inspiration on the parapets of Duino. Conceived in lightning as Winslow was—according to his mother, anyway, a summer thunderstorm, a freak event in the Coast Range. This too will go in the book. Everything will go in the book, everything Winslow knows or suspects, even the things half seen. Everything between the last eternity and the next. Oh, he was just warming up.

She wasn't there in class, though, not at first.

"Anybody seen Erika?" he asked, as casually as he could muster.

Nobody had, or nobody would admit they had, though Winslow did rate a scowl from Dave. He wondered what he had done. He expected he would find out.

"The Eighth Elegy," he said. "Seriously, you have to find a way into this. You don't have to like it, I mean, I really don't care—and you don't have to understand it completely, either. I hope not, because I sure as hell don't."

The expected little laughter rippled around the room. Then Winslow shifted into his sincere oracular semi-Biblical mode.

"This is greatness," he began.

But just then—ten minutes after the start of class—Erika drifted lazily into the room. She didn't notice she was late. She had to find a chair and get rid of her things and find a pen and rearrange herself while the rest of the class waited for her, and then she looked up at Winslow. Through a haze of something, drugs or drink, he saw a clear direct flash of hatred.

Winslow tried to start again. "The Eighth Elegy," he said. "What's he getting at here? What's Rilke trying to say?"

But all eyes were on Erika. It was her class now. It was her move.

"You know what I like about this?" she said. "Nothing moves. Nothing's got a body, nothing's got a penis. It's all so beautiful and *ethereal.*"

Winslow tried to think of how to answer this.

"I know it's what *you* like about it," she said directly to him. "I know you like them sensitive."

Winslow looked around the room and realized as he did—with a great wave of alarm and revulsion—that they all *knew*, that everyone in the room was on to him and Erika. What did they know? What did they think they knew? It didn't matter; what mattered was that the thing he had until now thought was private had been happening very much in public. He was one of them now, no better, no different: a foolish, fucked-up lover, a fifty-five-year-old teenager. His face flushed with embarrassment and rage.

"I don't know that this is helping anybody to understand these poems," he said quietly.

"Is that what this class is supposed to be about?" she said. "I thought it was the Dick Winslow show."

"Erika," said Dave quietly. She looked at him and Winslow saw that he had some kind of power over her, some calm, restorative influence. She shook her head like a colt settling down after a run and eased back into her chair. She was going to be good, for Dave's sake, not for his.

"OK," he said. "Rilke."

But as he looked around the room, to see if anyone had anything to say, he saw them all looking at him: the girls measuring their degree of disgust with him—his damaged head, his body, his fingers yellow with nicotine—and the boys, what were the boys thinking? Some mixture of the same disgust combined with a kind of perverse admiration. The boys liked them fucked up. The boys liked them unsober, untamed. Less like their regular moneymaking fathers and their sane lives. OK, Winslow thought. I've got the boys on my side, more or less. Next I'll revolutionize American poetry and after that I'll fuck the rest of the girls, two by two.

"You don't like Rilke?" he said. "That's fine with me. You don't like Charlie Parker, that's fine with me. But if you don't know Charlie Parker, you better not pretend you know anything about the saxophone. If you can't play Charlie Parker, you'd better not pretend to play. Because he's in there, he's in the music.

If you don't know it and understand it, then you don't know the music. You don't have to believe me. Like I say, it's fine with me if you don't. Maybe you can figure out some way to work your way into the music without knowing. I don't think you can but what the hell do I know?"

It was at this moment—a moment in which he had succeeded in interesting at least some of them again—when Erika reached into the gas-mask bag she used as a purse and rummaged around and finally found a pack of cigarettes and then, miraculously, a lighter. Without show—without even seeming to notice them—she lit a cigarette and then looked up. Dave was staring at her. Dave was giving her pity and terror, looking at the place where Erika used to be, the lost girl.

Dave loved her. Winslow had not realized that before.

Slowly she realized what she had done, reflected in Dave's face, in Winslow's, the others.

"Oh, shit," she said.

Erika gathered her coat, her bag, her scarf and hat and gloves and book and pen, and left. She had not realized. She had not meant to provoke; she had simply forgotten where she was, and this terrified her. Winslow saw it in her last glance round the room. His heart went after her when she left. He needed her. He had not had a chance to explain.

They were all looking at him when he looked up again: expectant, blank, like cows at a fence line.

"I can't compete with that," he said. "Let's go to the bar."

Later he finds himself alone again.

Later he finds himself alone in the apartment. The apartment which has, in the kitchen, false brasses for cabinet pulls and a floral band along the top of the walls, some kind of halfhearted country-kitchen motif. The floor is plain linoleum with a pattern of tiles printed on it—even pressed into it, a shallow indentation follows the edges of the printed tiles. But it's not meant to fool anyone. Nobody is meant to believe that the pot-metal chandelier over the kitchen table was ever made by anyone or cared about by anyone; the wood of the tabletop is so clearly wood-grain vinyl that Winslow understands it's not meant to trick anyone. No fool would mistake it for anything but itself: a picture of wood, printed on plastic and glued to a round of medium-density fiberboard. Not artifice but falsity.

The fake-tile plastic continues around the sink, along the

counters. The silverware is stamped stainless steel in an antique floral pattern, made in Korea. You can't even be sarcastic about this kind of thing. It's impossible to feel anything. The couches and chairs are at least good old-fashioned American vulgarity, ugly beyond belief but comfortable, some sort of nubbly baby-blue fabric. There is a picture of a duck on the wall, swimming in some willowy cattail swamp.

No one has ever lived here; they have only stayed, only temporarily. No one has even left any dirt behind. The expensive and thorough housecleaners—he paid for them in his security deposit—have eradicated any past guests and they will eradicate Winslow in turn when he leaves. The television sits in a colonial armoire, again made out of high-density fiberboard. These circumstances fit him more exactly than he wishes them to. He sits on the sofa with a glass in his hand as ever, speeding toward his own annihilation, feeling the rush of time passing. He's drunk, it's true, but the things he's feeling are true. He can feel the rush of time passing, speeding like electrons through his body, the passing seconds and milliseconds and microseconds and nanoseconds all lined up one after another and racing relentlessly forward. Nowhere to stop, no place to get off, until, of course, the grand exit—and even then in the wormy darkness time will race forward, with him or without him.

Winslow is thinking about June Leaf, about how he loved her in the sunshine of Mexico and how he loves her still, her long neck in the shade of a portico in San Miguel de Allende and Winslow across the way drinking beer under an umbrella. Somewhere under his skin and undying is his love for all these women: June, his mother, his first wife, his hundred girlfriends. And yet he is here alone. Some kind of gene he doesn't share, whatever lets people lead their happy placid lives; remembering Laurie and her sister and their seven husbands He's loved and he's been loved and yet here he is alone. For many years he believed that he had never really been in love, that he would be walking down the street one day and she would announce herself and he would discover that everything before was only play and preparation. Winslow no longer thinks this. He thinks that he has known what there is to know short of obsessive, crazy love and a little of that, too. And yet here he is alone.

Drunk: he goes over to the table where he was writing two nights before and sees the pages of scribbling there and remembers how grand it was all going to be. He's going to be a public joke again and not the private joke he has become. The widening gulf between the ground at his feet and the high immaterial undying plane of immortality—to which he does in fact aspire— makes him airsick, seasick, the pitch and wobble of the ground beneath his feet. Maybe he's just drunk but maybe the ground itself is giving way. He takes the papers from the table and he wads them up and throws them away, down with the coffee grounds and the empty cans of corned-beef hash.

Still the words stay in his head: *for Erika*, he had written. False hope springs eternal, as one of his students said.

The hallway's trimmed in the same floral band, up by the ceiling, the same baby-blue rug. The bathroom's lined with a dizzying triplicate of mirrors and there, dead center, is Winslow, smoking a cigarette. Looking at himself in his bandages as if that could prove existence or nonexistence. He puts the cigarette out and brushes his teeth and goes to bed, to wait there for sleep, for anything.

Spring came overnight, a Saturday in early March in which Winslow had gone to sleep with the winter wind whistling outside and awakened Sunday morning to the sound of water dripping from the eaves.

Some instinct sent him outside first thing and it was true: the air itself was soft and warm, although he could still smell the stale snow underneath. A message out of the South, an awakening, a smell of damp earth and sun, even at six in the morning. Something in him thrilled at the scent, the unexpected mercy. He had, apparently, made it through To what?

In the mirror his face looked closed and angry and piglike but the surgeries were healing. The radiation was not nearly so bad as he had been expecting; clean and clinical, it was hard to believe that anything had been done to him at all. The worst of that experience was over. The teaching was going well. He could call

up Laurie and have dinner with her anytime he wanted, he suspected—could have some fancy food and wine and touch her
breasts besides, a little pointless wrestling on the couch. He had
money in the bank and two months left on his contract here.
Really, things were not so bad. He remembered his feeling—he
first had it at Laurie's house—that they were a little family, that
he and Laurie were the mother and father and Erika the little
child, and for the duration of his breakfast Winslow relaxed into
this fantasy, knowing it inaccurate, not caring.

His briefcase was full of student work and there was Rilke to
be read and studied—really, he felt like he could use a few hours
in the library, another voice or two on the subject other than his
own—but this was spring, the first day. Spring was Oregon,
spring was love, spring was white wine in the damp grass. He
would not skip it for the library.

After a breakfast of sausages and eggs and toast—all bets
were off today, impulse and pleasure were king and queen—he
packed his fishing junk into the trunk of the Town Car and
headed out. Where? Someone had told him of a good small
stream, an hour away. Winslow didn't mind the drive, not on a
day like this.

He would take it easy on himself today. He would be good,
give himself grounds for the optimism that flowed so easily on a
day like this. Really, he wasn't so badly off. He checked the little
pile of pages on the table on his way out, the little growing pile,
and though the coffee-stained ones were embarrassing—he'd
had to fish them from the trash, the morning after—he felt like
there was a place in this world for him again. Life was possible.

He would take it easy on himself today. He had six cans of
beer in the little Playmate and six cans only; a canteen of water
and a pair of cheese-and-onion sandwiches and a banana to keep
them company. He had prescription sunglasses and a full tank of

gas. The road was bright with melted snow, and once he turned off the Interstate onto the two-lane it was like following a band of bright steel toward the mountains. The cows stood in the melting pastures in piles of their own shit, munching contentedly on hay, and the Pintlar Mountains shined like advertisements for themselves, sharp-toothed and glamorous. The only others on the road were slow-moving ranch trucks and flatbeds piled with firewood, the chain saws poking up out of the pile like weapons, the obligatory spotted ranch dog sitting on top of the pile. On a morning like this Montana seemed plausible; Winslow felt a tug of nostalgia—which he knew to be fake—toward these simple lives in this snow-clean landscape. To get up in the morning and simply work—to feed the cows and water the hay, or whatever they did—seemed like the height of luxury. And if the loggers' daughters he had grown up with turned out complicated and crazy, if they went toward Jesus or child-brides or whoring and heroin in Portland, that was because of the rain. Here, under these towering clean mountains, would grow simple uncompli-cated souls who would make each other happy and make the cows happy, too.

And I am the pope, he thought. Still it was possible to believe without believing on a day like this, the first spring day. Every-thing was fine here, as clean and high-reaching as the snowcov-ered mountains.

Around a final corner and there was Philipsburg, laid out so inconsequentially on a hillside. You could cover the town with your hand and still have miles of landscape all around you, the low hills to the right and the high rugged mountains behind the town, stretching south into the blue sky, blinding white in the sun. Green hills and wet black granite and wet asphalt shining like steel—it was intense, operatic. Winslow felt like this scenery was trying to put something over on him. Still, nobody made it.

It happened for other reasons. It would still be here when Winslow was long gone.

Turning from the two-lane onto a smaller winding road, he hoped that this road would not get worse than it was. He could track it with his eyes as it rose over the top of the hills. If there was snow, if there was ice, the lumbering Town Car would leave him in the ditch. And it was true that every other car was a truck of some kind with four-wheel drive and enormous tires. Many of them had big winches.

The road was fine, though—slow and bumpy but recently plowed and graveled. Up top was like looking down from an airplane at a hundred miles of mountains, hot white in the sunshine and snow. High-altitude cows watched him pass, and a herd of what he thought were elk on the south side of the road. It made Winslow feel like singing. Instead he lit a cigarette and started down into the valley. At the bottom of the hill was the bridge and here was the creek running under it, clear and cold and fast. It was more of a small river here, though you could easily wade across it in the places Winslow could see. He felt a mounting excitement looking at the water; this was what he was doing here, this was why he had come to Montana, this river, this day, these fish. Assuming there were any fish. There had to be fish. You could tell just by looking.

Winslow found a plowed turnout a little ways down from the bridge and parked and assembled his motley. The currents of air were running back and forth across the tight little valley, streams of cold air down from the mountainsides mixing with sun-warmed still air in the creek bottom. He saw the hoofprints where a moose had been, and the tracks of a hundred small birds. He saw the sun rising in waves off the surface of the snow, and felt its warmth reflected. He felt alive in every extremity, all of his blood up and running.

And this too would be taken from him. . . .

Through eight inches of snow he made his way back down to the creek, to a spot he had picked out from the road, where the water scoured a deeper channel running under the bridge. Which bug? Which fly? He started to tie a tiny Griffith's Gnat onto his tiny tippet but then thought, Fuck it. He was here to fish for pleasure and not for science. Instead he found a big greenish hairy thing that he knew should not work this early in the year and tied it on, a nice stout bug that you could see from Idaho, that would float on any current, and he tied it onto a nice stout leader that would not break—and probably would not catch any fish, either—and lumbered a couple of feet off the bank and cast his fly onto the water.

His first cast was awkward and short and dumped into a puddle of line and fly. But he was able to get the mess up off the water and timed his next cast more accurately, so that the line straightened and the leader straightened and the big greenish fly settled placidly onto the water a couple of feet above the hole, drifted down naturally and over and then almost over, and then a fifteen-inch trout came off the bottom and sucked that fly right down.

Subtle as a billboard, graceful as a flying mallet, Winslow reared back with all his might to set the hook and should have popped the fish right off. Somehow the stout leader held, though, and the fish was on fast. He was using an old soft four-weight and the fish was wide awake and fighting, down and running and then running straight at Winslow so he couldn't get the line in fast enough and then suddenly up in the air and furious. Why was it always called a *nice fish,* he wondered. Still this was a nice fish and maybe a very nice fish, bigger than he'd thought at first, a rainbow from the way he fought and maybe a big one. Sixteen or seventeen inches anyway. Winslow struggled to keep him off the bottom and out of the brush pile on the far bank, the rod bending and whipping, alive in his hands, Winslow alive himself.

When he brought the fish to hand—when he laid it on the bank to admire it and to work the bug out of its mouth—the fish was a nineteen- or twenty-inch rainbow trout. This was a big fish. This was the largest fish Winslow had caught in several years. He was about to throw him back in the water but decided at the last moment to kill him and keep him. He assumed this was legal. There was nobody around, anyway. He dashed the head of the big trout against a big rock on the bank and the silver body, the beautiful thing, shuddered and died.

He felt it immediately: his luck was leaving him.

Winslow tried to shake it off, to recapture his earlier force and optimism, as he trudged back toward the car through the snow. I will kill you and eat you, he thought, then I will go back to town and write the poems that will revolutionize American literature and after that I will fuck all the women.

But the feeling was gone, the fish was dead, and as he put it into the plastic bread bag in his trunk, as he slipped the silver body into the Franz wrapper and hid it next to the spare tire and closed the lid of the trunk, he understood that he had dared too much. The river gods loved their fish, sleeping in the winter cold, the sluggish near–ice water of late winter. The river gods would not mind if you took a little fish, or a whitefish, or if you were starving. But to take one of their darlings out of simple pride, this was asking too much and it would bring retribution. Winslow understood that these things—poems, women, rainbow trout— came as gifts from unseen forces.

He had offended his own muse and had to suffer as a result. Now he had offended the river gods as well.

It was all bullshit, of course, all wishful thinking. If there were gods out there behind the sky, they certainly weren't paying any attention to Winslow. But still he laid out the next cast with a disheartened feeling. He put the big silly bug over a deep pool under the bridge, cast it right out and perfectly into the current as it slipped past the bridge support, and then watched as a second fish, bigger than the first—bigger, maybe, than any Winslow had yet caught—the fattest, slowest, most deliberate trout he had seen in years, or maybe ever, came slowly to the surface after his fly and slowly circled toward it and examined it more closely and decided there was something he didn't like about it and gently, like a leaf falling, slipped back into the cold quiet depths of his hole.

It felt like simple justice to Winslow. He had sinned against his luck. Now his luck would have revenge.

He cast again, and again, to no avail. He walked a quarter-mile of bank upstream, pitching the big fly perfectly over fishy, fishy water, and nothing rose. He switched out to a complicated nymph rig—ten minutes of clumsy fumbling with freezing fingers and tiny tippets—knowing that the fly was not the problem, and it was not. The strike indicator was a bright-orange ball of synthetic fluff, a miniature Bozo wig that Winslow floated over every likely gravel bank and dropoff until he could see the negative image of the thing when he closed his eyes, a little green fluffball imprinted on his retina. Once in a while the bobber would go under to announce that he had succeeded in snagging a twig or a rock, twice so badly that he lost both flies and had to start over again. Once he tangled the whole rig up in a bush on the far bank trying to cast under it, and once he tripped on an underwater rock and fell sideways and wet his shirt up to the elbow. The day, which had been pleasant and fine in dry clothes, was much less pleasant with a wet sleeve. In fact it was cold, and getting colder.

After an hour of this he thought to himself, I can't even catch a fucking whitefish.

And on the next cast he caught a small ugly whitefish, with something wrong with its mouth. The river gods were fucking with him. This much was absolutely clear.

Winslow went back to the car and sat in the sun in the open door of the back seat and ate a cheese-and-onion sandwich and drank a beer and then another. If he'd had a can of beans and a can of spaghetti and a frying pan he would have mixed them up and eaten them together. If he'd had a fire-blackened grasshopper. If he only had a brain. He sat in the pale sun thinking about his luck: what he had done to spook his writing luck, which he indisputably had. Probably it was quitting his day job. You'd have to be awfully lucky to survive that. Somehow Erika had brought his luck back—something about suffering, the gods that Winslow knew about always wanted suffering. Erika: he thought of her and some awful foretaste came across his mind, some faint suspicion of what it would feel like when she died and he was still alive. Would it happen? Something.

Because he wasn't suffering now, not yet. He was missing her—Erika had skipped class the following week, he hadn't seen her in ten days—but he expected to see her again, he had every right to expect that much. And he expected that somehow they would talk again, they would drink and drive together. They would walk in the spring sunlight.

Maybe this was what he had been trying to remember.

Maybe they would not. An *inkling*, Winslow thought—what kind of word is that? But it was like a cloud had come across the sun, this sudden chill in his heart. What if she was not all right? What if she was already gone? She could be, he thought. He didn't know the medical complications but she was so slim, so frail. A drug experiment could put her over. A car crash, an accident of whim. She could do it to herself.

Winslow locked the car again and took his rod down to the water and started working downstream from the bridge this time, working some nice water on the far bank, but now he couldn't concentrate. Certainly it was all just imaginary, this whole line of thought; certainly there were no gods to play with him. But something was out there, in his bones he was sure of it. Every time he sat down to write and the writing came, he felt like his hand was being guided. The sitting down, the white page, the ballpoint pen, the discipline of every morning were just invitations to whatever came. And for a year now—two years—almost three, he had been inviting her and she did not come. Winslow was almost certain that, whatever it was, it had to be a woman. Not a girl but a woman. She had come when he had invited her and then she had stopped, and now that Erika was here, she had come to him again.

All ridiculous, of course. All fancy.

But something in here, Winslow was certain of. He did not make the river or the forest or the poem or the fish. He could not. He could receive these things as gifts; he could know where to look. But he needed her. In his instincts he was certain, the way the thing smelled. Out of the corner of his eye, he had almost seen her.

Winslow understood that he was wasting his time here. He wasn't going to catch any more fish. He'd be lucky not to fall in and drown. Before he left the river, though, he stopped his casting and fussing around and took a moment to look at where he was, to appreciate it: a little empty valley with a trout stream running through it, sunlight sparkling on the water, the redrock cliffs on either side. The evergreen trees farther up the mountainsides still held a dusting of snow and still higher up the snow was white and solid. OK, he thought: beautiful. But something else. Something was trying to get through to him, some little intimation.

Winslow stood and waited and nothing came. *Who if I cried would hear me among the angelic orders?* Nobody, apparently. Fuck it.

He rigged down and a literal cloud came courteously across the sun, darkening the afternoon to match his mood. A Forest Service truck rattled by and Winslow and the greenie inside waved madly at each other like long-lost friends reunited. How many different kinds of fool would he feel like before this day was over?

By the time he made it out to Philipsburg again the sky was threatening snow and the cooler was almost empty, a lone soldier left in the melted ice at the bottom. Winslow remembered the optimism of the morning and it was like another country; remembered the morning's promise that he would take it easy on himself and it was like another person had made it. Instead of turning for the Interstate and home, he drove up the hill and into town—the best kind of town, abandoned, moldering. Empty storefronts lined the main street like a mouthful of broken teeth. Houses, some inhabited and some empty, stood a uniform gray in the gathering afternoon dark, and at the top of the hill loomed the skeletal steel remains of some kind of mine. Winslow felt something like love stirring inside him as he drove the empty streets. He felt something like home.

The Central Bar was crowded and snug at four-thirty in the afternoon, a collection of gimme caps and old jokes on the back bar, a smell of frying hamburgers, a woman bartender of the biker-chick type—tight t-shirt, huge breasts, ratty blond hair and way too much eye makeup, over a face which could easily have belonged to a man, and a man hardened by experience at that. It was a style of bartender Winslow loved and one he hadn't seen in years. Where had they all gone? Who had taken the biker-chick bartenders and where had they taken them? But here was one, stranded in Philipsburg. She glared at Winslow when he first sat down—this would be her first response to everything new—but she softened into a smile as she approached him.

"What can I get you?" she asked.

Winslow unexpectedly found himself close to tears and it took him a moment to order. I want the whole lost world that you came from, he thought. I want my afternoons back, the ones I used to spend in the Pig. All gone, all lost. She was starting to wonder about him again when he managed to croak, "A bottle of Bud, please."

"You bet."

"And some peanuts."

He had spotted the peanuts on a big red beer tray down the bar, the rancher telling a lazy joke and cracking shells onto the floor. The whole lost world was opening up in front of him: peanut shells on the floor and cigarette smoking and afternoon drinking and why not? Everybody here had been up since five, everybody but Winslow. Everybody here had already put in a good day's work and it was Sunday besides. In their brown duck coveralls they stood with one hand on the bar and the other holding a cold wet can of Coors. Winslow had already marked himself as an elitist when he ordered beer in a bottle and by wearing khaki pants. At least he had not identified himself—by hat or clothing—as a fly fisherman. These were hardware slingers and worm drowners, if they had any time for fishing at all.

"You're from Athens?" the bartender said, shoving the bottle of beer toward him.

"I'm from Oregon, actually," he said.

"No kidding? How'd you get all the way out here?"

"You get visitors here."

"Yeah, but not in March," she said. "The skiing's over and the fishing hasn't started yet. Usually we get this time of year to ourselves."

"I'll leave if you want me to."

"You can stay," she said. "As long as you're not from California you can stay."

She took his money, kept the change, rapped the tip on the bar by way of thanks. The shake-a-day cup, the gallon mayonnaise jar full of money, the pickled eggs and pigs' feet floating like science projects on the back bar, the football pools thumbtacked to the walls, the smell of smoke and grease and hubbub of conversation: Winslow felt like he was home, or as close as he was going to get.

He was not home, though, or even close. And when it was time to drive home Winslow was drunk.

He stood on the sidewalk outside the bar taking in the cold clean sobering air and hoping for improvement. It had snowed while he was in the bar—not much—an inch—and he busied himself clearing the windshield and back window with his bare hand. He could feel the cold on his hand but somehow it didn't communicate all the way to him. The whiskey had not been a good idea, but he bought the first round and Debra and Robert, his new friends, bought the next two and he could not turn them down. Still it had been a bad idea.

The snow continued idling down as he left the lights of town behind. Like interference on a television set, somewhere between channels, the white specks and streaks drifting through his vision and making it hard to comprehend the road. In places it was easier to drive with one eye covered; it kept the centerline from wandering as much. The black on either side of his headlights and above was enormous and absolute, miles of nothing, an occasional ranch light off in the distance before the snow flurried up and hid it again. It was bad, bad. He hit the rumble strip a couple of times.

Winslow had always been good at driving drunk—he was naturally slow and cautious behind the wheel and so his instincts served him well—but not usually this kind of long distance. It was an hour back to town at least and time didn't seem to pass at all. He glanced at the clock and saw it read 8:45 and then drove for fifteen minutes more and it said 8:49. He would not have been surprised to catch it going backward.

What a thing to be good at, driving drunk.

The road snaked through a canyon and then, coming around the end of a turn, he found eyes in front of him, eyes shining in the headlights. Winslow stabbed at the brakes and discovered that the road was slipperier than he thought, slippery with the drifting snow, and then the car was drifting sideways and the headlights raked across the herd of elk that was standing, not moving, in the highway. Another fine mess, he thought, bracing himself.

Then he heard tires on gravel and felt the big Lincoln lurch and lurch again and then stop Winslow was standing on the brake pedal. He couldn't seem to make himself stop.

The car was ass-end in the ditch and sideways across the road. The elk—there were easily fifty of them and probably more—stared at him without curiosity and then resumed their unhurried journey from the mountainside to the river valley below. They were mostly cows and calves but there was one buck at the head of them that seemed to be speaking to Winslow in his magnificence. The rack of antlers towered above the rest of the herd, worn proudly. *You must change your life.* Always, Winslow thought, always the same message . . .

Gingerly he tried the accelerator pedal and felt the big car stumble forward, slip and stumble again and then he was on the road. He wondered if the car was hurt but he didn't want to stop, get out and check. What's done is done, he thought, and miles to go before I sleep. Just thinking that brought the stern Yankee judgment of Frost down upon him. Winslow, drunk, was ridiculous. And old Robert wouldn't go for ridiculous, he suspected; wouldn't like the looks of Winslow, or the smell of him. Well, he thought, Robert old boy: fuck you.

He threaded his way through the elk herd—they parted, shifted, came back together behind him—and down the road again, reinvigorated. Nothing like almost wrecking your car to perk you up. The whole thing a near-death experience. I want my angels, Winslow thought. I want my white light. Fuck, he felt good. No: great, he felt great. The road raced by under his wheels and maybe it was slippery, maybe Winslow would go for another little ride before the night was through, but he was un-killable. That was the thing he needed to remember: unkillable. He had forgotten and look what happened—the world always waiting if you let your guard down—the thousand kinds of trouble always waiting. But Winslow was back now.

Winslow was back.

What now? He would go and pick up Erika first. Whatever was going to happen next, he wanted her by his side. And then he would . . . keep teaching, sure, why not—it was only a couple more months and they were paying him thousands of dollars, not the untold thousands he was worth, of course, but thousands. The big American night was stretched out in front of him, just beyond his headlights, the roads that ran from here to

Florida, to Los Angeles, to Santa Fe and New Orleans and Memphis. He had always wanted to go to Memphis. He heard that Elvis's aunt was still living upstairs at Graceland. He had heard about Little Graceland which was the same as regular Graceland but a tenth the size, and also about Graceland II, which was some roadside episode of mental illness featuring every *TV Guide* that Elvis had ever appeared in, etc., and also the one partner—or was it the son?—who remembered the name and date of the original visit and everything that happened in that visit for every person who had ever walked in that door. Winslow wanted to find that boy and shake his hand: a memory even more useless than his own.

Now the time was passing. Now the time was going fast. He could hardly wait to get to town, to tell Erika about his new plan. And on the Interstate—the roads were clear and dry here—he had to set the cruise control on the Town Car to keep himself from going over the speed limit. Out here in the big American night with the big jeweled trucks rolling by and the moon, almost full, ducking in and out from behind the mountains and Winslow snug in the fat-ass seat of his fat-ass car. If there had been a gas station or store he would have stopped for a beer. He was done with good ideas.

All the way, he thought. If he knew anything about Erika he knew that she would go all the way.

Eleven by the time he pulled into town, eleven on a Sunday and everything shut down hard. Wind was blowing papers down the street and cop cars sat idling in their own exhaust, looking for somebody to bother, looking for Winslow. He drove cautious as a nun through the shuttered downtown, the traffic lights swinging overhead in the winter wind, and across the river of ice and through the sleeping neighborhoods, deserted, creeping along in the big car. Alone, at night, nobody out but him. The blue light of television shining through half the windows, or the yellow incandescence that still misled him into thinking that somewhere, somehow, somebody was having a happy family. A little reading before bed and then kiss the kids goodnight. Somebody somewhere was having a reasonable life.

Not him.

He saw that Erika's light was on, the miniature rundown house on the alley with its little fence and little porch. He had dropped her here before but he had never been inside. Winslow didn't belong here. He knew this but he didn't really feel it until he had shut the engine off and rested there for a moment in the dying warmth of his car. What was he there for? What was he in search of? He couldn't say exactly. He was after her, he knew that much. Something to do with her.

When he let himself in through the gate, though, he could see into the open window of the front room, and he saw that Erika was not alone. It was Dave, earnest redheaded Dave, sitting on the floor beside her couch, and Erika with her hand on his shoulder while they watched the television. They did not hear him.

He did not bother them.

Instead he stood in the cold outside and watched through the window and understood that there was nothing for him here. She was waiting, too—she was hoping, she was longing—but not for him. He stood remembering the spring day that he had felt that morning and wondering where it had gone.

"Did you fuck her?"

"Who?"

"What's her name," Erika said. "With the tits."

"You mean Laurie," Winslow said.

"That's the one."

"You know her name," Winslow said. "She knows yours, anyway. She seems to know a fair amount about you."

"I believe you."

"She cares about you," Winslow said. "She thinks you're wrecking your life. And she warned me not to try and talk to you about it, you know, about any of this because after that I'd never see you."

"Mom, is that you?"

"No," he said. "Not your mom, not your dad, not your boyfriend, not your doctor. I would like to be your friend."

"You didn't answer my question," Erika said. "Did you fuck her or not?"

Winslow looked into her face and thought that he had never seen such concentrated unhappiness. In his office with the door open, people passing by in the hallway outside, people listening—for all he knew—right outside the door. He imagined Laurie, Walrath, anybody. And yet it was impossible to be angry with her while he was being drowned in nostalgia instead, looking into her face, watching her slip away, like Portland, like June Leaf, like the old-lady apartment houses and bars, everything slipping away; wave after wave of the real false thing, the big self-indulgent fake emotion—poor me, poor me, pour me another, as the country song went.

"Close the door," he said.

"I have to go in a minute."

"Close the door," he said.

Erika regarded him skeptically for a long moment and then obeyed. She sat down in the old wooden office chair, all suspicion, and watched as Winslow brought the office bottle out of the bottom drawer. He set two paper cups on the desk and was getting ready to pour.

"None for me, thanks," Erika said.

"All right," he said. He put one of the cups away and poured a little for himself, just a little. It was not yet three in the afternoon and he still had to teach, a last class before spring vacation. It was in the air, the impending vacation. The students, all of them, were restless, distracted, excitable. Spring was whispering to all of them.

"I heard it was bad for you, actually," Erika said. "It turns out that drinking yourself drunk every night really kind of messes you up. You probably didn't know that."

"I didn't sleep with Laurie," he said. "I don't think it's any of your business but I didn't."

"You're right," she said. "It isn't any of my business."

Winslow looked across the desk at her and it was the old feeling again, the lost feeling. He needed her, she was going. He searched his brains for the magic words that would bring her back again, that would make everything all right again, but no such words existed.

"I've missed you," he said.

Come on, he thought, come on. And then he saw it: anger, and not indifference.

"You've been having fun," she said.

"I've been writing," he said. "You sure you don't want anything to drink?"

"What have you been writing?"

He hesitated a moment before telling her. Because talking about writing was a bad habit, a thing he quit long ago. But he wanted to reach her, to touch her.

"Poems," he said. And instantly felt pathetic. Here he knew that he had crossed some kind of boundary, he was someplace he didn't belong—because he never ever talked about his work until it had been read and finished and read again, until he had mailed it someplace, sometimes not until it had been printed. It was in his experience the worst kind of luck, the rally-killer of all rally-killers, to talk about a work in progress—and here he was using it as a conversational pawn, a way to keep this little girl talking to him. And she was little, he was always aware of it—the body of a twelve-year-old, so small and slight. What did he even want from her?

"I thought you quit with poetry," she said.

"When did I say that?"

"You were drunk one night," she said, and—seeing that she had scored a hit—she smiled. "Maybe I'll have a drink," she said.

Her antennae were working perfectly: as long as he wanted her there, she was always going away. Now that he wanted her gone, she was staying. He poured a drink for her anyway, unable to take back the offer. What had he gotten himself into? A sudden intimation: it was more complicated than he had thought.

"What's new?" he said.

"Nothing."

She sipped the whiskey, grimaced.

"You're writing again," she said. "That's new. How did that happen?"

For a moment he wanted to explain it to her. For a moment after that he just wanted to show her the new poems, so she could see for herself. Instead he shrugged his shoulders, turned his palms up empty-handed: it was a mystery to him.

He asked, "Are you doing any writing?"

"Never," she said. "I thought I was following you. The genre of silence. You know? where you just think about writing all the time and talk about writing all the time and you never get any writing done."

"Glad you like it."

"It's *way* easier than writing," she said.

Winslow had to laugh, though she was mocking him. Such a little bitch.

"What are you doing for the break?" he asked. "Are you going to Florida? Are you going to be on MTV?"

"Have you been watching MTV? All those chicks in bikinis, probably. What you want is a girl with a big front porch."

No, he thought—what I want is a twelve-year-old with a dirty mouth and a bunch of problems. And a boyfriend. He didn't say anything, just stared into his paper cup. What a small life it was, and shrinking.

"Are you OK?" she said.

"What do you mean?"

She touched her face.

"No, I'm fine," he said. "I'm more or less fine. I'm going to be fine."

"You look better."

"I'm not dying," he said. "I'm not dying quickly, anyway."

"There's a step," she said, and sipped her drink. Which meant she wasn't in any hurry to go. This watching, this careful gauging of his standing, made Winslow think that something was wrong with him. She was nothing to him, really. He remembered the two of them—Erika on her couch, redheaded Dave on the floor beside her—the two of them laughing together. And here he was, lugubrious and sad and slow. What did he have to offer her?

"I'm not doing anything," she said. "Sit around my house and get depressed, I guess. Nothing like a slow week in March. Maybe I'll take up snowboarding."

"I'd like to see that."

"You won't. What are you doing?"

"Nothing," he said. "Writing."

"Let's go someplace," she said.

He looked at her warily, sensing a trap. Already he felt foolish enough, fat and abject. I'll tell you anything, he thought. I'll do anything for you. And you know it.

But he did want to go. He could feel the little thrill when she said it.

"Where?" he asked.

"I don't know," she said. "Get in the car and drive. Can you get to Hawaii from here?"

"I don't think so."

"Can you lay off the advice for a week?"

MISTAKE MISTAKE MISTAKE his inner man was screaming at him. She was somebody else's girlfriend, somebody else's trouble. There was nothing in this for him but heartache and trouble—and this is what his inner man wanted, too, he wanted trouble. Maybe there was writing in it somewhere. Winslow had always felt nothing but contempt for those who couldn't write except in an emergency and now he was turning out to be one of those people.

"I can try," he said. "Let me think about it."

"What's there to think about?" she said. "We won't get another chance. Viva Las Vegas, come on."

"Let me think about it," he said again. But both of them knew, and both of them wondered. They were going. Where and why and how were all mysteries to be solved later, but they were going. Winslow felt his little heart doing tricks in his chest. They were going.

Man and telephone: Winslow in his kitchen again. A March night was sighing and sobbing in the trees outside his window, inconsolable, hysteric. He was supposed to have been at Laurie Fletch's house for drinks a half-hour ago.

Some kind of strange paralysis had come over him. Or not-so-strange. In fact, his old friend on-the-one-hand, on-the-other. On the one hand, he was ready for adult company, and Laurie was clearly that. On the other hand, she was having a few fellow members of the faculty over, and faculty was not exactly what he had in mind. He could hear the puns and complaints already, the savaging of the Provost and the salary structure, the new movies and new restaurants. Somebody would like each of them and somebody else would have tried them and found them wanting. On the other hand, there would be whiskey, cigarettes and hors d'oeuvres, all of which Winslow was in favor of. He would be out of the house. He would be in the company of those he was suitable for.

It felt quite literally that he could not force his body to move. Each time he started to his feet, to get his coat and start his car and drive the seven blocks to Laurie's, he found that he could not will himself to go. He stayed in his chair. On the other hand, when he had definitely made up his mind that he was not going to go, when he had determined absolutely that he was going to have a placid night around the house, to watch television and have a drink or two, then he found himself seized with an insatiable restlessness, a driving, nerveless inability to sit still. He drummed his fingers, lit cigarettes and then put them out forcefully when they were only smoked halfway down. An observer would have seen expression following expression across his face: uncertainty, followed by definite intention, followed by puzzled passivity, followed by surrender.

And all this time he never left his kitchen chair, except to pour himself a drink. A little drink, in case he was going to drive over to Laurie's house in a minute.

Really on the other hand was Erika. He was supposed to pick her up in the morning, to drive somewhere and do something, it wasn't clear where or what. It was supposed to be an adventure, and although Winslow in principle approved of adventure, he felt a little queasy as this one loomed. Somebody else's girl, a nice round thirty-five years younger than he was. But really it wasn't that. Part of him wanted to go, for reasons he didn't understand, and part of him didn't, for reasons that made perfect sense. And somewhere in the middle, missing, was the man who was supposed to decide.

Winslow was losing himself again.

He recognized the feeling, and it scared him. At the same time, like an old friend, whispering to him again: it was all right, all he had to do was let go. Easy to slip, easy to fall. Let others make the decisions for a while. It was hard being Winslow, harder than it had to be. He could just let it slide, see where he might end up. Let the others do the moving and shaking. Insoluble—why not admit it? This big engine of desire that ran the world, three billion people and everybody wanting something, everybody trying for theirs, everybody but Winslow. He couldn't even decide if he wanted to get out of his chair or not. He wanted drinks, he wanted cigarettes, but that was automatic. Nothing real to decide.

But whether to go to Laurie Fletch's house was beyond him. Maybe, maybe not. Lots of reasons on every side. And the thing is, Winslow thought, the thing that nobody wants to talk about is how good it feels to just let go. He felt his lips and shoulders relax, just sitting there. He felt a pleasurable warmth run up along his spine, a *lassitude*, he thought. I'd like a double lassitude. Who would find him? Who would come for Winslow, to discover him marooned at his own kitchen table, the victim of his own indifference?

Erika would.

Serve her right, he thought.

And it was this little spit of venom that propelled him into motion. Out of the chair, into the raincoat, down the stairs and into the car, all at once, like he was running from something. Because she didn't deserve it. She was just somebody who happened along, somebody in the path of the big baby Winslow. Fuck them if they didn't love him enough. Fuck 'em all, said the big baby.

I'm going crazy, Winslow thought.

But *crazy* was just another word, he knew that by now, another way of getting through the day. His problem was something else. What? Driving to Laurie's in the wind and the rain, he felt that he belonged outside with the wind-whipped trees, the last melting rotting patches of old snow. He felt all wrong.

He pulled up in front of her house in the big Lincoln and parked a couple of houses down the street and shut the ignition off and the lights. The windshield blurred immediately with rain, big drops falling through the trees that made a splattering sound. The impulse that had carried him this far had spent itself, and he felt the confusion seeping back. No. Not confusion—he knew what he felt, he just couldn't make it add up. What was he supposed to do? She knew. He remembered Erika on the cold steps of his apartment, her face cold and blue. He thought of her and felt something give way inside him.

A tapping at the window.

He looked up, and there was Laurie at the passenger door, out in the rain, staring at him through the rain-splattered window. He opened the door for her and she got in, dripping.

"Are you all right?" she asked.

"I'm fine," he said.

He sat there staring out the windshield, avoiding her eyes, feeling them on his face.

"I was out smoking," she said. "I saw the car pull up and I . . ."

"I'm sorry," he said. "I'm just having an odd night."

"What's the matter?"

"I don't know," he said.

"Do you want to come in?" she said.

"Do I?"

"Probably not."

"Is Walrath there?"

"The whole gang," she said. "In a festive mood, too. I suspect you don't want anything to do with them."

"You're probably right."

"Then why'd you come?"

He had to look at her then, turned to see her face—her long, thin, worried face—in the streetlight, crazed and shattered by the rain on the glass. Winslow had been right about her: She knew what he was talking about. She had been there before.

"I just got restless," Winslow said. "I was hoping, you know, if there weren't too many people . . ."

"You didn't even come in."

"I was going to."

She looked at him gently in the half-light, then put her cold hand on his wrist.

"Poor you," she said. "Poor Richard. You've had a terrible winter, haven't you?"

"I've had worse."

"Tough guy," she said. "You know that's wrong."

"It works all right," he said. "Till it quits working. How are you?"

"I'm fine," she said. "Come tomorrow if you don't want to come in tonight. I'll be all alone and lonely."

"Oh," he said.

"What?"

"Oh, I'm going on a trip," he said.

"Where?"

"I don't know."

"With whom?"

"I can't say."

"Oh," she said, and took her hand back. "One of *those* trips."

Winslow looked to see if she was laughing at him but she wasn't. She was looking into his face, trying to see something there. She was weighing him, testing him.

"You're really not from our tribe, are you?" she asked. "You're really some other kind of different person altogether.

For a minute there, I thought I understood you, but I don't at all. Do I?"

"I'm sorry," Winslow said. "I didn't mean to bother you. I'll let you get back to your party now."

"I didn't mean to scold you."

"It's not that," Winslow said. "I'm just having an odd night. I'll be better tomorrow."

This was the moment, he knew it as it came upon him: the moment in which he would turn to Laurie, would hold her in that slow embrace that he remembered from her sofa. She wouldn't come to his apartment now but she would come later, after her guests had gone home. He knew it just from the wrongness of the two of them, huddling in the rain in a damp-smelling car while the others drank and talked; the two of them in the car alone. *Turn,* he told himself. She was nervous, true, and thin, and anxious. But she knew him, a person his own size, in mind if not in body. He didn't know what would happen with her but he knew the door was open, he could just walk through it, they would be sane and decorous and adult. He saw it in her eyes: this was the moment, they were the people.

But the paralysis crept over him again, and he could not move. He turned a quarter of the way to her and he could turn no more. She saw it in his face, he saw it reflected in hers: the wrongness, the inability. Literally he could not move farther.

"All right, then," Laurie finally said. "Have a nice trip. I've got to get back to the throng."

Winslow felt something tear then, something finally broken in him. It was not too late. But still he could not turn.

"I'm sorry," he said.

"Sorry for what?" said Laurie.

But she knew. He could hear it in her voice. She opened her

door and then, at the last possible second, she turned back to him and kissed him on the forehead.

"Be careful," she said.

"I will," he said.

"You won't," she said, and laughed at him. "But you really truly ought to try."

Just then a gust of rain blew through and Laurie shrieked, in a comic way, and slammed the door and darted for her own door amid the pelting rain. Winslow sat just as he had: turned a quarter of the way toward the empty place where she had been, a puzzled, attentive look on his face. Something was wrong with him. What? He sat for minutes, pondering, without coming to any definite conclusion. Then slowly drove home.

The next morning at six, on a cold March day, when Winslow stood in the doorway with his leather valise in his hand and the Town Car idling outside, he felt, turning, looking back into the apartment, he felt that he was always leaving. He was sick of goodbyes. Always moving on, always trying to improve himself by the geographical method. Looking back into the dim light of the apartment, he knew that there was nothing to recommend it, nothing for him here, and he was coming back. It was only ten days' trip.

Still, he was leaving and he was tired of leaving, starting over and he was tired of starting over. Other people were having lives. People in his old hometown were still there, still married to whoever they got married to. Though it would be, he thought—perched between the nowhere of the apartment and the cold and gray of a cold spring day—a total bitch if this was where he ended up when the music stopped. Take me to Honolulu, he thought, an idea which propelled him out the door.

Ten minutes later, at the door of Erika's little house, he was confronted by a different mood. She was not there, for one thing. He pressed the doorbell button and nothing happened—he could hear nothing even with his ear pressed up to the window. He knocked and knocked. He tapped on the glass. He understood, then, that this was all an elaborate setup to fool him. There was a camera somewhere, to capture the foolish look on his fat face. It was funny, if you thought about it.

Finally she came out of the back room, still asleep in her underwear and t-shirt, her legs an awful sight, her face like an unmade bed. She was alone, apparently. She let him in without a word and went back to her bedroom, leaving him in the cold gray light of her kitchen. It was just light. Her house: a student palace, walls lined with books, a reproduction of a Frida Kahlo painting big on one wall, which made 100-percent sense to Winslow—the one with the nice big dripping wound in her chest and the crown of thorns and the delicately beautiful face, yes sir. Relentless reminders that she was twenty: the two hundred CDs by people Winslow had never heard of, the refrigerator pictures of parents and pets. This was indisputably a bad idea. He had no business here, none at all. Her problems were of a different order and a different kind.

Erika finally came out of the back room in black jeans and black t-shirt, mangy and yawning.

"I fucked up last night," she said. "Sorry."

"What happened?"

"Oh," she said, "nothing."

"What does that mean?"

She looked at him skeptically, deciding whether to answer or not. Big Dad wants to know. Big Dad wants to make sure no fun was had.

"Stayed up late," she said. "Drank a little too much. I sort of forgot. Can you make some coffee? I'll go get ready."

"Where's the coffee?"

She waved her hand at the kitchen counter and disappeared into the bedroom again: a bag of coffee, already open and some of it spilled on the counter, a German coffeemaker. Like all neat people, Winslow didn't understand messy people or how they lived their messy lives. At least he didn't have to live with her. But what was he doing here, then?

An hour later they were on the Interstate and she still wasn't talking and Winslow still felt like a fool.

By that afternoon they were in Idaho, driving south. Winslow stopped in some naked little town and bought whiskey and cigarettes for Utah. He couldn't remember what the regulations were exactly but he wanted to be prepared. She still wasn't talking. She stayed in the car looking unhappy, half asleep, as he ducked into the liquor store and bought two fifths of Johnnie Walker from a woman dressed as an old whore, rhinestones and wrinkles. Winslow fell in love on the spot.

The little town asleep under towering snowcapped mountains. There would be a library here where Winslow could sit by a window and read and listen to the cars pushing slush around in the street, the footsteps of pedestrians in rubber boots. It was so simple, what he wanted.

By three in the afternoon they were slogging through Salt Lake City and she still wasn't talking. A hundred miles of bad traffic, everybody blond. After Montana and Idaho they had moved back into money-world and Winslow was amazed at the BMWs and Mercedes and shiny pickups everybody drove. Once in a while a Mexican family in a K-car but mostly it was a hundred miles of money and bad temper and everywhere the same landscape rolling by outside, EXXON WENDY'S PIER ONE BURGER KING SHELL TARGET INTERSTATE BANK and COSTCO, they must have passed a dozen Costco's driving south, like the old cartoons in which the mouse is running and the same background passes by time after time, door-couch-lamp, door-couch-lamp. . . .

"You want to go back?" he said.

"Why?"

"You don't seem especially happy to be here."

"I'm not an especially happy person," she said. "I'm not having an exceptionally happy day."

"What's the matter?"

"Nothing," she said. "I stayed up too late and drank too much. I feel fucked."

"That's one way to put it," Winslow said—just to let her know that he was officially annoyed with her, as she was with him, apparently. In mutual annoyance they drove south and south, past the Mormon Eden under the mountains, the city and then the smaller towns trailing off like echoes until the last town was in the rearview mirror and NEXT SERVICES 28 MILES ahead of them. The scenery opened out and flattened and the day started to leak out of the sky; open desert stretched on either side of the highway. The cars were older and the trucks took over the road, pushing along in lumbering convoys of ten or twelve or twenty semis. Just at dusk—which was early, four-thirty—the setting sun burst out below the deck of clouds and sent a yellow blast of light across the desert floor and in that light the gray of the last few months turned to color and Winslow realized that it was not always everywhere gray. Portland was gray in the rain, and the snow in Athens and the overhanging clouds, the houses and dead lawns were all gray, the cars, the faces of the people you passed in the street were all gray. Now they were going somewhere else.

Without asking, Erika reached into the back seat and opened one of the bottles of Johnnie Walker. She passed it to Winslow after taking a long drink from the bottle directly.

"We should stop soon," Winslow said.

"Where are we going?"

"Where do you want to go?"

"I don't know," she said.

"Maybe we should figure that out," he said. "We can stay on the Interstate and go to Vegas, we can cut off down the road here and go to Tucson, maybe go to Mexico. We can pick up I-10 there and go to Miami if you want, although we'd never make it back to school in time. Whatever you want."

"I want you to decide," she said. "I don't care."

"We could go to L.A."

"No," she said, "definitely not L.A."

"Where to, then?"

"You're driving," she said. "You decide."

Winslow would find out sooner or later, what was wrong with her, what was wrong with him. This was his idea, more or less. This was his fault. And in some way, even if Erika was going to be a pill, he was glad he came. He would have come this far just for that flash of light, that moment when the color came through the screen of winter. They were playing baseball down in Arizona. He had never been to a spring-training game. They were drinking beer and getting sunburns. He felt the old pull of the road, anywhere but here, anything but this. If he were stuck in Arizona he realized that he'd be moping after snowy days and rain but he had not been stuck in Arizona. He had been stuck in Athens, and as near as he could tell the nearest thing to a nondepressed person there. Laurie said that except for Belva the department chair, every woman she knew was on antidepressants. It was, she said, the end of sex as we know it.

Not, apparently, the end of sex in Utah. The woman behind the counter at the Days Inn in Beaver, Utah, eyed Winslow like a bona-fide child molester when he came in to register for the room. She looked from his damaged face out to the car where Erika sat slouched back with her feet on the dashboard. It was dark out, the early dark of winter, but the big bright lights were on in the portico of the motel, and in them Erika, looking tiny and dead.

"Two double beds," he said.

The clerk looked again from Winslow to the girl.

"I'll have to see some ID from her," she said.

Winslow was ready to give her the finger and walk; then remembered that he was far from home and by now a little drunk, the next town miles away, the next motel unknown.

"I'll be right back," he said.

And this was the part he didn't want, the explaining-it-to-Erika part, her sitting there steeping in her own bad mood for the twelfth hour in a row. Surprisingly, she wasn't angry; she handed over her wallet without complaint, and Winslow brought it inside. The clerk scowled at the tiny picture on the driver's license and then squinted to see Erika out the glass doors and then back to the picture and then back malevolently to Winslow.

"I guess that's all right," she said, in a voice which clearly conveyed her opinion to Winslow that the world would be a better place without him. Soon enough, he thought, soon enough. And what kind of a world was it in which poets have credit cards? A certain lack of discrimination, he thought.

The gigantic room with the two enormous guilty beds. Erika and her little ratty gas-mask bag, curled into the chair, under the lamp, watching television.

They went out searching for dinner in the tiny Utah town and found a lone Chinese restaurant sitting in the glow of its own pink neon. Even on Saturday night the parking lot was near-empty and the smell coming out of the back was not good: grease and some kind of powerful cleaning agent.

"I'm not going in there," Erika said.

"Fine with me."

They drove around and around again and the choice was the Chinese place or McDonald's. The town seemed completely asleep except for the McDonald's and the Dairy Queen, where high-school boys and girls stood under the streetlight, freezing in the March night.

"What do you want to do?" he said.

"You decide," she said. "I don't care."

At long last Winslow was completely fed up with her. He drove them back to the Chinese place in complete certainty that it would be awful, that they would be lucky to escape with their lives and health. But Erika would hate it, he knew, and he was interested in that.

Inside was water and a green plant—killer feng shui—and a lot more of the same grease-and-cleaner smell. There was one other table occupied in the whole place and no alcohol on the menu. If Erika had looked less ostentatiously appalled he would have pulled out then and there but he wanted to punish her. Winslow needed her. She could at least cooperate.

"What do you want?"

"I don't want anything," she said, throwing the closed menu across the table at him.

"I'll have the Kung Pao chicken," Winslow told the waiter, "and she'll have the fried rice with tofu."

Even the waiter looked dubious, as if no one had ever ordered food from him before.

"What to drink?"

"Tea," Winslow said.

"Beer," Erika said.

"No beer," said the waiter.

"Beer," Erika said again.

The waiter stalked away, went back into the kitchen to spit in their soup.

"That was charming," Winslow said.

"I don't feel charming," she said. "I don't feel the need to charm. What are we doing here?"

"We're having a nice dinner," Winslow said. He could feel the whiskey simmering inside him. He said, "We're having a nice conversation at our nice dinner. Wasn't that a nice drive today?"

"Fuck you."

"And aren't you splendid company."

"As I said," she said.

"I know," he said. "You don't feel charming."

"Never mind," she said, and turned from him to stare out the window, where there was nothing to look at. Winslow's car in the parking lot. He studied the decor: blood-red wallpaper and hanging lanterns, plaster Buddhas painted gold, plastic imitation of oriental fretwork; or maybe it was real wood, the place certainly seemed old enough. Like everything else in the universe, the place filled him with nostalgia for a simpler, better time, a feeling which was, however, complicated by the fact that he had never eaten a decent meal in a place that looked like this. Never once.

"My mother used to work in a place like this," Erika said. "Right when we first got to the States. I never really figured it out but we ran out of money for a while, my dad did, and she had to get a job. It was the worst."

She said it all without once glancing at Winslow, without

ever taking her eyes from the window, but still he felt examined. What should he say? What did she want? This was completely unlike her.

"What was so bad about it?" he asked; and this seemed to be the wrong question—she turned and stared at him with contempt. She had thought better of him. He had proven himself a fool.

"What?" she said. "You haven't heard about the plight of the Chinese daughter-in-law? These guys in the kitchen, they had to have somebody to feel superior to. And there was my mother with her big tits and her Polish accent."

"I didn't say it wasn't bad," Winslow said.

"About the ten-thousandth time somebody makes a joke about dog in the soup," she said.

"I'm not arguing with you."

"You don't even see," she said. And it was true he didn't; he had that feeling—so common in his life—that an ancient argument was being played out with Winslow for a bystander. Who she was fighting with, what she was fighting about, had nothing to do with this particular time, these words said or unsaid. He was somewhere near to the core of her anger but it was veiled, unclear. He wouldn't get any closer.

"What was she like?" he said. "Your mother."

He knew he was taking a chance—he saw it in her eyes as she took a long while making up her mind to answer, or not—but it seemed like a moment. And maybe it was.

"She was an awful person," Erika said. "She was selfish and mean and crazy. She fucked her way out of Poland and never loved anybody in her life. And I'm just like her."

"I don't think so," Winslow said.

"But you don't know what you're talking about," Erika said.

"Let's just go now, you want to? Go back to the room, have a little drinky."

"I'm hungry," Winslow said.

"Oh, but you're always hungry, aren't you?"

"It's true," he said, "except when I'm smoking. This place looks like it might cure me."

"You're incurable," she said. "You just want to take everything in your mouth and swallow it whole, you want it all inside you. You're a monster, Richard. You ever get to Tokyo, Godzilla better watch out."

"I want everything," he said "It's true."

"And I want to get out of here," she said.

Just then the bustling waiter, hurrying and harried despite the empty seats, brought Winslow's food out and rushed off for Erika's. It was candy-apple red, this alleged chicken, and gave off a strange aroma. Always a disappointment, Winslow thought, to find your expectations so fully realized. Erika looked across the table at his plate with undisguised triumph, she was right, she was always right, this was awful.

As usual Erika pushed the food around on her plate. As usual Winslow polished his. Then as usual—or so it felt—they paid the apologetic waiter—Was he the cock, too? Was there anybody else behind that red door? Was that him yelling at himself in Chinese?—and went back to the motel room to get drunk.

The clerk glared at them again.

The pictures were in their same places on the walls and Erika was slugging down scotch like there was a time limit. Everything was happening again, nothing was happening new. Another fake environment like the apartment back in university housing, and for a moment Winslow thought that he had never left, that he was trapped inside this new nowhere, clean rooms with polyester spreads on the bed and safe anonymous nonart in frames on the wall and nothing in between but the asphalt tundra: MCDONALD'S SHELL PIER ONE SEARS BEST BUY BARNES & NOBLE.

The new nowhere.

He poured a plastic cupful of ice and then of whiskey and sat down heavily in the scratchy plastic chair. How many motel rooms? How many barefoot trips to the ice machine? A momentary saddening glimpse of the memory of June Leaf damp in her bathrobe, Winslow's slippery dick inside her. Whatever else was going to happen here, that wasn't it.

"You know who I want to be?" she said, flipping through the channels with the remote.

"I give up."

"Emily fucking Dickinson," Erika said. "Didn't spend a fucking minute worrying about what anybody else was doing. Got her work done."

"Died a virgin."

"Died a virgin, that's right," Erika said. "How drunk was I when I was talking to you about that?"

"Drunk enough."

"Jesus Christ," she said. "How drunk will you have to be before you forget about it? Or at least stop talking about it. It was just an idea, for fuck's sake."

"Did Emily Dickinson curse like a drunken pirate?" Winslow asked. "I was just curious."

"Oh, fuck you," she said.

"Where do you want to go, anyway? We should figure it out tonight."

"We'll be thinking better in the morning," she said, waving her glass at him, then sipping from it.

"That's what I mean," he said. "Where's the fun in that?"

"I'll go wherever you want to," she said. "It's all new to me."

"If we stay on the Interstate it will take us to Las Vegas."

"Which is what? A bunch of tourist crap, isn't it? I've never been there but it sounds like hell."

A new fire started in Erika's eyes, some new insult she had registered.

She said, "This is all a test, isn't it? You're trying to get me to make a fool out of myself. It's like your fucking music."

"No."

"You know where you want to go," she said. "Take me along. Feed me drinks and read me poetry and I'll be fine. You're dying to get off the Interstate."

"It's true."

"So get off the Interstate. You don't care what I think."

She drank again, a little more vigorously.

"I don't even know what I'm doing here," she said.

"I'll drive you back," he said. "Anytime."

"Too late to stop now," she said. "There's nothing on TV."

Then it was midnight or maybe after and Erika was drunk. "I was the one who found her," she said. "In the bathtub. She meant for me to find her."

"Nobody would do that," Winslow said.

"You didn't know her."

"But nobody would do that."

"She said she would before that. She said she was going to do it every year, once or twice a year she'd get drunk and tell me all about it. When I was little she said she was going to take me with her."

Winslow felt a shiver run up the back of his neck, somebody stepping on his grave.

"You have to forgive her," he said. It sounded false and stupid and bad even in his own ears—bombastic Papa and his all-purpose advice—but he knew somehow that he was right.

"That's easy to say," she said. "Easy for you."

"I don't know if I could do it."

"What the fuck are you talking about?"

Winslow could see it clearly but it kept vanishing as he tried to close his hand around it, kept turning to air and slipping away. He was still certain but he couldn't put it into words.

"She's not here," he finally said. "She's not *going* to be here. All that wasted feeling, you'll never get it back."

This didn't make sense to either of them but she tilted her head, trying to hear what he meant.

"Being angry with dead people," Winslow said. "It doesn't make any sense. It's just suffering. There's plenty of suffering. You don't need to make more."

"She's not dead," Erika said. "She's still alive, in here."

She tapped her head, exactly—Winslow noticed—where his own wounds were healing.

"She talks to me every day," Erika said. "She tells me that I'm shit, that her own life would have been fine if she never had me. I can either talk back to her or I can believe her. She's not going to shut up. That thing she did, she meant it for me. I was the one who was supposed to find her."

Winslow felt a chill again at the sight of her face, like a woman looking down a long empty tunnel. He momentarily suspected her of drama but it wasn't true. Whatever else Erika believed, she believed this absolutely.

"Fuck her," Winslow said quietly. "Let the dead bury their dead."

"We get drunk," Erika said, "but we never have any fun. How come we never have any fun?"

There was a new light in her eyes, a new ferocity.

"Let's do something," she said.

"What?"

"Something," she said. "Anything. Anything but sit around and talk about our problems. Look," she said, "look at this."

She went into the bathroom of the motel and Winslow had the feeling he should stop her. But he was huge and slow and drunk, a bag of water, nothing. She was back before he could start, carrying his old-fashioned safety razor, fumbling it open.

"Watch me," she said.

Erika took the blade out of the razor and laid her hand flat on the table and drew the blade across the back of her hand, inscribing a neat flat line across the skin. Nothing at first; and then the line turned red, and welled up, and the blood started to seep out of the side of the cut and down onto the wood-grained vinyl of the table.

"That's something, isn't it?"

When she looked up Winslow saw that there were tears in her eyes.

"That's not nothing," she said. "That's something. You can feel that."

She handed the blade to Winslow. He took it at first and then dropped it quickly, as if it were poisoned, as if it were red-hot.

"This is not for me," he said.

She held her hand in the air, admired it. A drop of blood fell onto her jeans.

"Feel it," she said. "Feel it."

(All this emerging the next day in impressionistic dribs and spatters, clearing into memory out of dream but slowly, blurred around the edges, the purple fog of alcohol slowly fading into black and then into light again, the blue light of the television, the only light in the room . . .)

"Feel that," she said, and took his hand and pressed it to her bare stomach, and Winslow felt it: the knot under the skin, the lump of something. Instinctively his hand tried to pull away but she kept it pressed there—the tight drum of her belly, the suppleness and elasticity of her skin reminding him of how young she was.

"What is it?" Winslow asked.

"I don't know."

"Why don't you find out?"

"I don't want to know," she said.

And then, one last moment before the curtain descends: Winslow holding an imaginary steering wheel, turning it an inch to the right.

"Just like that," he is saying. "Just that easy."

And even as he is saying it—this is where the shame comes from, the burning stupidity and the knowledge of it—he knows that he is in part saying this just to impress her, just to show the little girl that he can be dangerous, too. Making a lie out of himself, a story. Remembering as he is telling his lie the face of Nelson Brightwater, the sunlight on the waxed floors of the day room.

Sometime, though, he had cut himself or she had cut him. Somewhere in the fog at the end of the night before. The bandage sat on the back of his hand as a reminder.

They drove south on the empty two-lane highway, past miles of nothing, empty plains of sagebrush, gray in the winter light. That flash of color, Winslow thought, where was it? He had seen it the night before, that moment of return to light, to life, but it was gone again. The clouds hung steadily in the sky; the hills absorbed the light and gave back nothing.

Erika slept in the back seat. Winslow drove with the radio off and a tumbler of sweet milky coffee for company. They had crossed some kind of line the night before and neither of them was easy with the other.

He passed a battered sign which read PHOENIX 485. It took him a moment to figure out that these were miles, that this battered empty highway with its old motels and bars was once the main road south. Here, where Winslow belonged, in the abandoned country of the past. Carry me back to 1948, he thought; take me to the Pendleton Round-Up, find me a cowgirl, move out on the ranch. Either that or head for 52nd Street, go the opposite direction, go see Charlie Parker, go see Billie Holiday. The old motels clustered in abandoned-looking towns with miles of nothing in between. The old motels with the old aluminum umbrellas—striped in yellow and rust—lined up on the concrete apron of the pool.

She had been naked and next to him on the bed when he awakened that morning. Winslow was in his usual boxer shorts and undershirt but Erika had been naked. He could still feel the press of her body, so hot and light. He felt surprise at first and then guilt, as he lay next to her without moving, almost without breathing, trying not to wake her, just for the luxury of her touch. So tiny and light. He wondered how she had gotten there, what they had had in mind, late and drunk and angry. Why were they always angry?

Mountains gathered on the horizon and the road rushed to meet them, red cliffs with white snow at the top. Red and yellow and black, the canyon colors. Winslow started to feel the excitement. This was somewhere new, somewhere he hadn't been before. Somewhere in the last thirty miles it had turned beautiful; still harsh and cold, still flat under gray skies, but beautiful. It was like music, the way the sage flats gave way to mountains, the horses standing in the open ground, the few spare houses well away from the road. Something about the houses especially, their humility. They did not try to keep up with the sweep of the landscape but sat modestly behind their own fences. It felt to Winslow that he was driving away from something, going down a road that ended ahead. No cars overtook him, and only an occasional ranch truck going the other way.

That cut on his hand, though: it had been seeping blood all night when he awakened, as had the cut on Erika's hand, so that the sheets were streaked and splattered with blood, some of it dried brown, some of it still fresh and red. He wished that he could think this inconsequential. He wished that he could summon any kind of lightness or humor, but it was far from him, too far to go.

Driving, he remembered the shock of standing—coming out of the comfortable haze of lying with her, feeling her next to his body—getting to his feet and looking back still hazy and seeing her naked and smeared with blood. Certainly things were going further and faster than he wanted. Really he ought to take a right, drive her to L.A., drop her at her stepfather's house and let her be somebody else's problem for a while.

Winslow didn't want to, though. He didn't know why but he didn't want to.

Somewhere near the edge of the Navajo reservation the hills came straight up to the side of the road and the red cliffs stood overhanging and grim and beautiful. The road began to weave through an enormous empty landscape and Winslow felt his heart rise in his chest at the sight of all the open space. Something inside him answered to the sight. Something rang. Where he was, the road was still in the shadow of the clouds, but ahead the clouds were breaking up into seas and armies, sunlight chasing cloud shadows across the plains and mountains. The road took him to the edge of a wide empty valley and looking down he felt like Jesus: the world opened up in front of him, his for the taking. But Winslow didn't want the ground, he wanted the air, the miles of empty space in front of him; wanted to drive his car right off the edge and fly into outer space.

Something answered: some empty place inside his chest that exactly matched this emptiness outside. That was equal.

Winslow had the feeling long before he came to name it but even then the name came as a surprise: he was *happy*. He was not right to be happy but he was. Some combination of this place and this trip and Erika asleep in the back seat had conspired to make him happy and now here he was. He did not wish to be elsewhere or otherwise. He wished to drive like this forever.

Fenced sagebrush pastures of Navajo sheep and ten-sided hogans next to decaying trailers and still nobody on the road. Winslow put his sunglasses on so nobody would see he was weeping. His little heart was wrung out inside him, flipping and turning the way it did when he heard a piece of music, a woman's voice especially, Billie Holiday's take, for instance, on the second chorus of "All of Me" . . . He fought the urge to wake Erika up so she could see it; she might like, she might love it, but Winslow had learned through long experience that perfect moments were fragile things and easily wrecked. He didn't dare change anything. The happiness coursed through him, the feeling of grace.

Also he had written something that morning, a little something. He didn't know if it was any good or not—he never knew until well after the writing—but it was enough to justify his continued existence for a day. He had gone out quietly, trying not to wake her, looking for coffee, confused as they come. The motel was by the side of the Interstate but the real town was a mile away, you could see it from the motel parking lot, standing behind a windrow of bare-branched poplars. He drove in slowly, little edges around everything, little rockets and stars in his eyes. In town he found his own memories and dreams inscribed in wood and brick and iron. His own childhood stood on Main Street except that here the street was called 100 West: the brick school, the playground with its great long teeter-totter and swings. In the center of town—the buildings all lined up primly together like children at a fair, afraid of getting separated—stood what appeared to be a working Mode O'Day store, still in business after all these years. The C Penney's had gone out of business but left their sign behind, the usual thrift store taking over the building, the ancient Easter dresses in the window. The downtown still had a working hardware store and also a grocery store—a primeval Safeway in the airplane-wing design—and the Snow White café, where Winslow ordered ham and eggs and hash browns.

Fat and kingly Winslow sat and watched the ordinary life around him: the families on their way home from church, the ranch hands done with morning chores and in town to talk. It was cool outside, almost cold, and the café heated up with the smell of bodies and coffee and steam and grease. Winslow the lone outsider watched and listened, read a left-behind section of the Salt Lake City paper, eavesdropped. A lifetime's worth of regular. Winslow knew he'd blow his brains out if he tried to live like that but from this distance it looked attractive: home, security, safety, sameness. Everybody knew everybody. He sat waiting for his food—the kitchen was backed up in the after-church rush—and remembering in the smell of the place his childhood, again: the cafeteria food and floor wax and ancient conversation. They were all still there, back in Jewell, living their lives without him.

He had his little pad of paper in his pocket, and his mechanical pencil. While he waited he set the paper in front of him on the table and waited to see if the words would come. *Dear Erika,* he started—as everything started lately, he would write these words at the top of the paper and then erase them later. But she was the one he wanted to explain himself to.

"Pull over," she said from the back seat.

"What?"

"Pull over," she said. "Now."

Winslow found a turnout by the side of the road, the start of a dirt road that ended in a gate, and pulled the big car off. As soon as it stopped moving she was out and vomiting. There wasn't much—there couldn't be much, she had eaten only a piece of dry toast that morning—but she couldn't seem to stop. Her small body, hunched over, heaving. Winslow didn't know what to do. He sat in the car with the engine running and then he shut it off and got out. She waved him away. She didn't want him anywhere near.

The air had changed, though. Something was different. The red dirt under his feet, the smell of it, something. It was still cool but something was coming.

When she was done he said, "Are you all right?"

"Fucking perfect," she said. But then she grinned, and shook her head.

She said, "I don't know how you do it."

"What?"

"The late nights, the drinking. You must be made of iron."

"Are you OK?"

"I'm fine now," she said. She looked around at the red cliffs and long views, the tattered sky, the sun trying to break through.

"Where are we?"

Winslow shrugged.

"Arizona, Utah," he said. "Somewhere in between. The Grand Canyon is over there someplace."

"And what are we doing here?"

Winslow laughed. "Beats me."

"I just thought since you had all the answers . . ."

"Let's go," he said. "If you feel OK."

"Let's go."

Out on the highway Erika slouched on the far side of the front seat. Winslow willed her closer, remembering the touch of her from that morning. Had anything happened? It seemed unlikely. He didn't remember sex but he didn't remember anything else, either.

He held his hand toward her, across the expanse of upholstery, the hand with the bandage across the back.

"I don't remember this," he said.

"Oh shit, Richard. Did I do that?"

"I don't remember."

"I'm such a fucking idiot," she said. "Why do you put up with me? Why does anybody?"

"I don't put up with you," Winslow said. "I enjoy your company. I don't know why but I do."

"I don't know why, either," she said. "It's a total fucking mystery to me."

She balled herself up on the seat, arms wrapped around her legs, and stared off out the window; and Winslow, sinking, saw that he had depressed her again. Somehow he could not explain himself. Somehow he had turned slow and plodding and earnest. The lightness of heart, the soaring he had had ten minutes before, was gone entirely, and in its place was earnestness.

At least they were moving, though. At least they were going. He didn't know where but they were going. Erika was with him.

Flagstaff: a bar full of French bikers who were taking turns on two rented Harleys and a ten-passenger van all through the Southwest. A nothing, nowhere bar down the street from their antique motel, the blood of Route 66 still faintly pulsing there. The French bikers, all decked out in leather and fringes, looked to Winslow's eye 100 percent homosexual but apparently they weren't—black mustachios and lots of shoving—tequila and beer and sometime in the night Winslow seemed to remember three of them lifting Erika onto their shoulders and she stayed there calmly drinking a glass of beer while they drank beer beneath her.

The road down into Phoenix with a crippling hangover, cloudy in Flagstaff, where it was still March at sixty-five hundred feet, and then grinding down the elevation mile by mile until the sun came out and the desert started to blossom. Winslow wished he knew the names of the flowering and leafy plants, the surrealist scribble of branches, the portly cactuses. Fifty miles outside of Phoenix they got stuck in a traffic jam for no reason, stopped cold. Winslow put the beast into Park and rolled the windows down and the hot breath of the desert came pouring in the windows, the perfume of a hundred strange plants and the feeling of heat and clarity.

"It's like some kind of paradise," Erika said. "It's like a different world."

And Winslow, stuck in traffic with his sunglasses on and his head throbbing in time to the music, couldn't feel it. Lumbering and slow and dull.

Straight through Phoenix in the teeth of the afternoon rush and then the question: left or right or straight? San Diego, Tucson or Mexico?

"I don't want to go to Mexico," she said.

"What's wrong with Mexico?"

"I don't have a driver's license," she said. "I mean I've got, like, a student ID and that's it. I don't think they'll let me into Mexico."

Winslow absorbed this for a minute. Then he said, "You drove home from the bar the other night."

"I didn't say I couldn't drive," she said. "I can drive fine. I just lost my driver's license. I mean, I've still *got* a driver's license. I just don't know where it is."

"Well, that's reassuring," Winslow said, imagining himself trying to prove to a highway patrolman that she wasn't actually sixteen. No, officer, I'm her uncle. Thank God for cruise control but no more driving while not absolutely sober, he thought.

"So Mexico's out," he said. "Right or left?"

"Right is what? L.A.? San Diego? I don't think so."

"Left it is," he said.

I-10, downtown Phoenix; heading east through the smell of orange groves and it was like a dream coming out of Montana, the gray light replaced by warm and glowing skies and smells. Winslow still didn't know what he was doing here but it didn't matter. He was ten feet tall and bulletproof. The sun was fading in the western sky and cars full of Mexicans drove by and fancy rich cars and everybody in the last glow of the sun and it didn't matter. Even his mistakes were correct.

"*Because women who want to be* artists shouldn't have husbands or babies," she said. "It fucks them up."

A motel room somewhere, drinking gin with the door open and the wind sifting through palm leaves outside. Somewhere in the desert.

"Because I don't know why but it does," she said. "It's true! You look at the lives of these women they start off fine and then nothing. Either that or they're like sixty and publishing their first books. I mean I'm sure that's perfectly fine for somebody but I don't want to be sixty and have all my work in front of me. Plus it sucks. It's like *Driving Miss Daisy* or something."

"Is that it?" Winslow said. "That's not it."

"Don't tell me what I think."

"Why not?" he said. "It's fun."

"Exhibit A," she said. "We're just talking about it and you

won't let me say what I think. It's always something more complicated or something better that you thought up. And we're not even married."

She sipped her gin, tilted her head sideways, looked at him through narrowed eyes.

"You don't even realize," she said. "It's part of the air you breathe, everybody breathes. The whole world has told you since birth that you know better than me."

"That's not what I said."

"No, but that's what you meant."

"No," he said. "What I meant to say was you were lying. You don't care about this political bullshit. That's all that public thinking, all that expected emotion that you got secondhand someplace."

"Thank you, Professor."

Fuck you, Winslow thought—but he didn't say it, he still couldn't bring himself to say it to a woman. He swallowed the impulse, lit a cigarette, regarded Erika through the haze of smoke: a blunt unbeautiful face, the pipe-stem legs curled under her. But Erika was wearing shorts and some kind of abbreviated shirt and her skin was fine and white in the yellow lamplight. Her blue wolf-eyes. Winslow felt his dick stir at the sight of her. Why not? But he already knew why not: because she didn't want to.

"There's something else," he said. "Some secret reason, out of the daylight—the real reason, the thing you feel."

"Exactly," she said. "I don't even feel the right things according to you."

"Erika," he said calmly. "Come on."

He looked at her through the haze of his smoke and she looked levelly back and they held their gaze steady until Erika broke down and laughed.

"You lose," Winslow said.

"Fuck you."

"Are you going to tell me?"

"A drink from now," she said. "Two drinks from now. Why are you right all the time? It's fucking annoying."

"I exist to annoy you," he said, staring at her legs in the lamplight, touching the scab on the back of his hand.

Texas at an even seventy-five miles an hour, exactly five miles an hour over the speed limit. New Mexico in the rearview mirror, and Winslow, with a feeling of physical dread, behind the wheel as ever. The dread came from the hangover and also from the not-knowing. He knew he would have to retrace every mile he was driving now, and—while the miles he was racking up now seemed fine and adventurous—he suspected that by the time he was trying to get back to Athens in a hurry, things would not seem so exciting.

Erika was staring out the window, bored or thinking or both. The scenery didn't offer much here: scraps of cloud, a general gray dullness with low hills off in the middle distance. After Arizona it was like switching from *War and Peace* to somebody's laundry list. Sometimes Winslow thought it was nothing more than the weather: blue skies for good feeling, gray for bad. If he had been born five hundred miles south, in California sunshine, he would have been happy and successful and smart instead of the brooding imbecile he had become. He remembered some girl telling him that she was a real Oregonian because she didn't mind not being able to feel her feet and fingers. A little chilly and clinically depressed, Winslow thought: my kind of gal.

He reached down to drive the radio for a while, turned it on low volume and pressed the search button—untrustworthy machine—and watched the digital numbers spin around and around again. Nothing. They were out of radio range on the FM side anyway, and Winslow didn't want to hear the cow and pig reports, the middle-aged rock and accordion love-and-death in Spanish on the AM dial.

With his fat fingers he advanced through station after station of noise with Erika sighing busily beside him and twitching in her discomfort. Here they were, driving off the edge of the world, and still she needed to make her preferences felt: what she wanted and nothing but. He found a fading pop-rock station out of El Paso and a blasting FM signal out of Mexico but he went farther down the dial, where the educational stations were supposed to be, without any real hope; and then, as happened to him sometimes when he gave up hope, Johnnie Hodges came suddenly out of the speakers, "Black and Tan Fantasy." Again it seemed to Winslow that he was living in a wonderful world, a world in which the black pearls of Harlem could shine across space and time to here, which, if it wasn't the middle of nowhere, you could at least see the middle from here. Winslow sat back into the smooth luxury of the music, the miles passing effortlessly.

"This is a test, isn't it?" Erika said.

"What?"

"This shit on the radio," she said. "It's a test, right? And I'm supposed to fail."

"Believe it or not," he said, "I actually love this."

"And if I was a better person I would love it, too," she said. "I know that and yet I don't give a shit."

Winslow started to laugh, which made her mad again.

"You've got to stop," she said. "You always win."

"I don't know anything," Winslow said.

"I know, but you act like you do."

"Welcome to adult life," he said. "Pretending. You know, I was in high school in this little town in Oregon, maybe junior high, I was pretty young. And my father had worked the whole time we were growing up at this one mill, pulling green chain, and then after a while he drove a forklift in the yard. Big guy, shot-and-a-back kind of guy. And then, this one year, right before Christmas they shut the mill down, like a week before Christmas. And I came home and he was in the kitchen in the middle of the afternoon, which he never was. I thought somebody had died or something. And then I saw that he was trying not to cry. I don't think he ever actually did cry in front of me but I could see that he had been crying."

"What's the moral of *that* story?" Erika said. "Don't be a girl no matter what."

"No," Winslow said. He let a couple more miles drift by before he spoke again; something about his mood and hers, something crossways and tired, made him wish he hadn't started this story. But Erika was waiting. He saw the picture in his mind of his father's shoulders, slumped and tired, the smell of chicken in the oven, the sound of the rain falling on the wet leaves outside and the free-fall terror in little Richard's chest. How to explain.

"It felt like he had been taken from me," he finally said. "It felt like my father had been stolen away and there was this other man standing there, you know? And I know now that it wasn't like that, he had both things in him, it wasn't one thing or the other, you know, the big strong father or this little shrunk-down guy, it was all in him. But this was like the one day where he couldn't pretend. And always after that I knew it was all pretend. I never trusted him after that."

"How very nice of him to fake it," Erika said.

Now Winslow was genuinely angry with her. He had given her a secret, and she had spurned it. They drove in silence for a while, an animated silence in which each of them argued with the other, or rather with the tiny homunculus of each other that they carried in their heads.

A few miles down the road Erika said, "There wasn't a lot of pretending in my house."

A few miles later she said, "Look, I'm sorry about your dad and all."

"That wasn't exactly what I was trying to say," Winslow said. "I was just trying to make a point, is all. I wasn't trying to make you feel sorry for me."

"I know," she said unhappily; then, unexpectedly, came scooting across the expanse of seat, lifting the armrest back into the middle seat and sat next to him, close to him, touching him— resting her bare hand on his arm. A quick lucid rush of desire ran through Winslow. He wanted to sleep with her. It was suddenly clear in a way it had not been before. This was not within the rules and not part of the trip they had started out on and he did not think it would happen. Until a minute ago he would have said that was all right with him. These were the terms they had started on. But now here it was again: desire.

"There wasn't a lot of wholesome pretending in my house," she said. "There was some lying."

"Not exactly the same thing."

"That depends on the angle," Erika said. "Sometimes they're pretty close. Let's take my stepfather, for example—all the time my mother was alive he would pretend, he would live as if she loved him. Then she would get drunk and tell him how much she hated him. Then they would go back to pretending again. Now the party line is that he always loved her, and she always loved him. All these nice big emotions."

"You like honesty."

"You don't?"

"I don't know if I've ever seen it," Winslow said. "As soon as you say, I'm like this, or, I'm like that, I feel like you've already told two lies."

"What's the other one?"

"The I," he said. "The one thing that you are."

"Whatever you say, teach," Erika said.

And at that moment Winslow understood: they were not arguing about whatever they were arguing about, which he could form no clear picture of anyway. This was all about something else. What? He didn't know, he wouldn't. Erika let her hand rest on his arm for a minute or two longer. Then, as if psychic, as if she could hear his little dick crying out to her, she dropped her hand to his thigh and left it there, apparently indifferent, staring out the windshield at the gray unfolding monotony of West Texas as Winslow drove on, quivering lightly at her touch.

"*It's the circle,*" Erika said.

They floated side by side in the jacuzzi at some motel in Texas, eleven at night, all alone. In fact Winslow had found the lights and shut them off so nobody else would bother them. It had been raining all day, still March, still grey, and some part of it lingered in Winslow's chest: the low clouds, the cows standing in mud by the side of the road. A dinner at some roadside chain restaurant—Denny's? Wendy's?—which even Winslow had a hard time with, and as usual Erika continued to kill herself. He had the feeling—dangerous as ever—that no matter how much he drank he couldn't get drunk. He tried to pace himself but the scotch went down like water.

"It's like, if you're inside," Erika said, "you have to believe in it. You fall in love, you have a baby, you love the baby, the baby loves you, everybody has to keep the ball rolling. It's like that's real, love is good, no questions. Jesus Christ, I'm fucked up."

But Winslow was all ears. This was the real thing, the little depressive heart of the matter.

"Tell me," he said.

"No," she said. "Because I'm just going to find out that I'm wrong. I always do."

"I'll shut up."

"You'll never shut up."

She sighed, and lay back into the warm water. She was apparently willing to admit that she had a body to this extent, even to enjoy it. A little bee of lust buzzed around in Winslow's head, a little aimless bee.

"Everybody's holding hands," Erika said.

Winslow waited for the rest of it but it didn't come for a minute or two. In the meantime some dim Texan poked his head into the dark pool-room, saying "Hello? Hello?"

Neither of them answered. In time he went away. When Erika spoke again it was like she was talking to herself.

"Somebody lets go of somebody's hand and the circle gets broken," she said. "Then you've got to close it up again. Either that or you get stuck outside, you know? and everybody's holding hands but you. Dear God, stop me for I am babbling."

"This is what you really think."

"This is what I really think. That's why you've got to stay outside. You get in the circle and you get caught, you have to stay there, you have to keep repeating the same lies as everybody else."

"Who said they were lies?"

"OK," she said. "If you're in the circle they're not lies. We all live for each other, we all help each other out. I don't want any part of it. Love makes the world go round. What the world needs now is love sweet love."

She said these lines with such contempt that Winslow felt his own heart shrivel and shrink inside his chest. What if she was right? Snares and delusions everywhere. Everything he lived by.

"It's worse for women," she said. "I know you don't want to hear it but it is. It's fucking death."

But Winslow, lying in the warm dark water, heard her words not so much as her voice; and in her authority, her certainty and anger he heard the voice of the full-grown woman she did not want to become. In the dark she came to him full-bodied and full-breasted and hungry as she would never be. But he could see it, he could imagine her so. She was right, of course she was right, she felt what she felt and lived as she lived and Winslow was nobody she needed to apologize to. But remembering the lump in her belly and the ropes of her arms—remembering the cuts and bumps and carelessness—Winslow couldn't help feeling angry in return. Why wouldn't she do him this one small favor? Why couldn't she want to live for his sake if not for hers?

The circle, again. In this Erika was right. He wanted her inside the circle.

In the dark he pictured her coming to him grown and fully ripe and it seemed to him that they were destined to be together in that form in some other life; not this one, worn and used up as it was. Some afterlife in which they might begin again without history. Too much had happened already here, the years and miles and failure clinging to Winslow, the dead mother who wouldn't let go of Erika. Maybe she was right; maybe it was better to let this one go and take their chances on what came next. This seemed on the face of it insane but probably no worse than what they were doing now. Or maybe the same as what they were doing now.

"That's what I like about you," Erika said. "You're outside. You don't care. You and Emily Dickinson."

"I'm not exactly a virgin," he said.

"You just think you're not," she said. "You're worse than me. Nobody's ever going to touch you."

"It's not true."

"That's why you write so well," she said. "You see things clearly."

"I only write about the things I love," he said.

"Maybe," she said.

And again in her voice Winslow heard the woman she would not become, felt again in his memory the lump in her abdomen, closed his eyes again and saw in the dark the full-grown woman coming for him and that pulse of desire. Strange to get it that way, through her voice. But there it was, his little untrustworthy dick rising underwater, rising toward her. He knew what he wanted, he wanted what he wanted, although he knew that it might be better if he didn't. Cautiously he reached his hand to touch the warm wet skin of her thigh, and she let him. He expected her to pull away but she didn't. He felt the wet warmth of her body, afraid to move his hand, afraid she might notice, but then he heard her breathing in the echoing room and he knew she felt it too. Winslow let his hand inch higher on her leg and she didn't stop him. Everything happening slowly, inch by inch. His hand rested where the elastic of her bathing suit met the skin of her thigh, just resting there, as if it had landed there by accident. She didn't stop him. Winslow could feel the heat of her through the thin fabric of the suit. She was disembodied no more. She was breathing with him and her breath was hot on the skin of his neck. He could feel her as she shifted toward him, just a quarter-inch but toward him, and opened toward him, and kissed his neck.

"Hey, who turned the lights off in here?"

It was a Texas drawl as loud as a Klaxon horn and immediately afterward the neon lights jumped out at them all bright and green and the two of them separate again and blinking in the hard light.

The lady clerk was angry with them. "Those lights are *not supposed* to be off when the pool is open," she said. "I could have a liability."

"Fuck you," Erika said quietly.

"What?"

"She said she was sorry," Winslow said. "Really, it was my idea."

"We're closing anyway," the clerk said. "Closing up the pool. Y'all have to run along anyway."

She looked from Winslow to Erika to Winslow to Erika— Erika standing there shivering in her towel like an abandoned twelve-year-old—and then back at Winslow and slowly shook her head. Erika deliberately picked up her plastic cup of scotch and ice and slowly sipped from it. That's my girl, Winslow thought—throw a little gasoline on that fire, why don't you? The clerk shook her head again.

"I'm on my way," Winslow said. He pulled a t-shirt over his wet skin and it stuck, wrapped his towel around his wet bathing suit and only then noticed what the clerk had already noticed, that he had a great huge prong hanging out the front of his wet suit.

Too late to stop now. He waited in the doorway for Erika, wilting under the angry headlights of the clerk. Erika took her time, of course. No hurry, no worry. She carried her flip-flops instead of wearing them, leaving a trail of wet footprints behind her.

"Poor Richard," she said, in the hall outside their room. "Is your brain giving you trouble again?"

"It's not my brain," he said. "This time."

"I know it's not."

He slipped the magic card into the lock and opened the door and let her in and then followed her. As the door slipped shut she pushed him into the room and up against the wall. She kissed him quick and hot on the lips and then knelt at his feet and slipped his wet swimsuit off him and took him in her mouth. When Winslow tried to touch her she pulled away. She shook her head. She didn't mind touching him but she didn't want to be touched. She went at it furious and fast; she wanted to take care of him and get it over with. This was exactly what Winslow wanted but not the way he wanted it at all. He tried to pull away but she wouldn't let him. Some part of him didn't mind. He wanted to touch her, wanted to lie next to her and kiss her breasts, but this was all he was going to get. And then he saw that she was further away than ever and retreating fast, whatever he wanted, this was the opposite of what he wanted and it was still too late to stop and his body wanted this, anyway. His body felt her hot mouth on him and his body liked it and when he felt himself starting to come—good girl—she kept her mouth on him and didn't flinch. And Winslow felt as lonely as he had ever felt. Why had they come so far? Only to wind up further and further from where they wanted to be. Where Winslow wanted to be, anyway. Her face was hard and angry and bright when she looked up but Winslow could see the start of tears in her eyes, too.

Panama City, Florida, four days out of Athens in the rain. Two-lane highway along the Gulf, a slow mistake, miniature-golf courses and discount swimwear outlets in the rain.

Erika said, "Ah, the redneck Riviera."

Winslow said, "This is nasty."

Jeeps full of college students in the rain in their bathing suits, big breasts and good teeth and blond hair, a million dollars' worth of regular, Winslow thought. I like Chevrolet and baseball. I like TV.

"Where are we going?" Erika asked.

"Why are you asking me?" Winslow said. "I haven't known for days. Maybe we should get back on the Interstate."

"So we can get nowhere faster."

"Exactly."

"I want to look at the ocean," Erika said. "I've never seen the Atlantic."

"How about the Gulf? It's a lot closer."

"That's what I meant," she said. "You know what I meant. Then we can go back if you want to."

Winslow heard these words in a strange way, they struck him wrong and resonated inside him. Of course they were going back. Of course this had to end somewhere. But to hear her say it so bluntly, so callously, was in some strange way traumatic. In the way a dreamer who is being called back to waking will fight and cling to the dream as long as he can and wake up reluctant and still tattered with cobwebs of the dream . . . Of course they were going back. There was no way around it.

"I want a Coke," Erika said. "I feel horrible."

"Of course you do," Winslow said. "What were you expecting?"

"Well, I was hoping for better."

"The triumph," he said, "of optimism over experience."

"I don't have quite as much *experience* as you."

Ending, he thought, in bitterness. Everything ended in bitterness. And they had never even genuinely begun. He thought of the long miles back to Athens, the long dull days. Soon enough they would be going home. Soon enough this would be over.

The children were all out having fun here, all the springbreakers from Ohio and Tennessee, and Winslow wondered again what evil whim had brought them here: the great tans and frisbee players, the rap music beating out from their tiny cars. America at play, everybody liking what they were supposed to like, everybody but Winslow. They came around a corner in a traffic jam of Jeeps and Volkswagens and there was the Gulf, flat and gray in the rainlight. Still, it seemed to shine.

"Look at that," he said.

"Well," Erika said. "There it is."

Her voice when she spoke sounded so flat and airless that Winslow felt his heart sink again. Why shouldn't she be out there with the other fun bunnies? Why should she be trapped in this old-man car with this old man? He was wrecking things for her, he understood that. She should be out there in the Jeeps, out in her bikini and suntan.

"We can stop if you want," he said.

"No," she said. "Get me out of here."

"You don't want to go to the beach?"

"I abhor the beach," she said, "except in the rain. And even though it's raining, this still looks too much like the beach to me. Let's keep going."

Winslow looked at her sideways—keep going where? keep going why?—but she wasn't giving him anything: feet on the dashboard, her little body half sideways in the seat. Windshield wipers keeping time. My sad song, Winslow thought. He kept going, as she wished.

At dusk they were out of the happy part of the coast and down to Apalachicola, a little dirty-looking town in the rain. They found an old motel of the type they favored: a little faded and very cheap, with rocket-shaped lampshades and strange switches by the edge of the beds. They went out looking for the Gulf at sunset and found that it was too far away—across a causeway and out to a barrier island a couple of miles offshore. The water between the mainland and the island looked shallow and gray, a couple of lonely oystermen tonging their way across in long flat boats.

"We'll go tomorrow," Winslow said.

"Whatever," Erika said. "I don't care."

"Come on," he said. "You can do better than that."

"I'm tired, Richard. I don't feel too good. I'm not especially perky, OK?"

"No," he said—and didn't say anything more, didn't follow up, because he didn't know how to say what he wanted. She was shrinking on him again. Sometimes the regular full-size person and sometimes the little girl; and when she was the little girl, he knew he had no business with her. As now.

"We can go back to the room."

"Do we have anything to drink? I want something."

"What?"

"Scotch is fine," she said. "If you've taught me nothing else, you've taught me to like scotch whiskey. When you first gave me some, back in your office? I thought I was going to throw up."

"You didn't look like it."

"I was trying to impress you."

They stopped at the ABC on the way back to the motel and got a bottle of Johnnie Walker, then detoured through the downtown—short streets clinging to the water, boats in people's yards, the smell of garbage everywhere, of rotting fish and salt water—looking for someplace to eat. There was nothing happy here, no trinket shops or putt-putt golf courses; a working port down at the end of every street. I could live here, Winslow thought, I could be happy here. Assuming he could be happy anywhere. Assuming he was interested in being happy. He recognized this place: the place where nothing quite made sense, where he didn't know what was going to happen next, didn't know what to steer by. Who would take care of him this time? He had no one now. The public mercy, the public hospital.

Whatever was coming next.

They found a bar, a waterman's bar, comfortable although

odd-smelling. Erika ordered a beer and the waitress didn't blink, a good sign. Winslow tried to order oysters but they were out.

"What do you mean, out?" he asked.

"We don't have any," the waitress said. "We only have them fresh and right now we're out."

"OK," Winslow said. "Give me a minute."

"I'll get your beers," she said.

"I like this place," Erika said. "It feels real."

And even though he had been thinking the same exact thing a moment before, Winslow felt compelled to argue with her.

"Everything's real," he said. "Watching television is real. Going shopping at the mall is real."

"Bull*shit*," Erika said.

Just then the front door of the bar slammed open and an oysterman in hip boots came through the doorway bearing a heavy burlap sack dripping with seawater. He carried the thing the length of the bar and into the kitchen. When the waitress came back with their bottles of beer she said, "Looks like we have oysters now. How many?"

"Two dozen," Winslow said.

And Erika said, "See?"

"See what?"

"You know what I'm talking about."

"Oh," Winslow said, and drank his drink instead. All this arguing and to what end? Some fundamental buried thing, some deep disagreement. Everything else was just symptomatic. But he couldn't seem to stop himself, the big fussbudget, the professor.

"Everything is real," he said. "Everything is just as real as everything else. If you can touch it."

"You don't even believe that yourself, Richard."

That haggard look on her face, he thought. That sense of urgency. Something was happening here, something more than he understood.

"It's irritating," Winslow said. "Everybody thinks that real life is somewhere else now. Nobody wants to live in the world we've made."

"Maybe there's just nothing to talk about."

"People are still living and dying," Winslow said. "People are still falling in love, even at the mall. Somebody will fall in love with somebody today at the mall someplace in America."

"I'm sick of you, Richard," she said. "You don't even believe what you're saying, you've just got to disagree with me."

"That's why people want to read about the black people now," he said. "The Indians, the rednecks—anybody but the people who are reading these books. They can't stand their own lives."

"Oh, fuck you," she said.

She stood and looked around, as if to make sure that everybody in the bar was watching, which they all were—threw a glass of ice water in Winslow's face and walked out.

There were not many people in the bar, perhaps a dozen, working-class people from the looks of them, and they were all staring at Winslow. He picked up a napkin and wiped his face and then used Erika's napkin to wipe the front of his shirt. They were expecting him to go after her, he could feel it, but where could she go in a town this small? Winslow was in no hurry. The waitress came up nervously to the edge of the table.

"That's all over," he said. "I'm very sorry. There won't be any more trouble."

"That's all right. As long as she's not coming back."

"She's not coming back."

"You still want your oysters?"

"Just one dozen," Winslow said. "I'll have a barbecue sandwich, too."

"Sliced or pulled?"

"Pulled. Outside if you got it."

"We've got it," the waitress said. "Don't you worry."

After dinner—dinner and two more bottles of beer—Winslow went looking for her. Erika had been right, as he knew she was all along: this place was right, the food was good, nobody was trying to impress him with any of this or fool him, either. A spring night but warm. People out driving around with their windows down in their cars. Montana seemed like a dream to him then, a kind of uniform gray haze. The idea that Montana was somehow his real life and this was not seemed wrong to him in a kind of amusing way. Where was he? Going, gone.

Erika was not at the motel, which made sense, as she didn't have a key.

Erika was nowhere in this nowhere little town. A Tuesday evening in mid-March, sleeping. Kids gathered outside the Dairy Queen under the streetlight, like moths, bouncing off each other, laughing. Every street ended in water, the smell of fish and salt water and two-cycle oil. Winslow wandered the three blocks of Main Street and then the docks, where a crew unloaded a fishing boat under big worklights. It was mysterious, the way they were working at night, the way the big fish—Winslow had no idea what they were—came up out of the hold on a conveyor belt like they were coming up out of the belly of the ocean itself. A big dead shark lay on the deck. While Winslow watched, the conveyor belt stopped for a moment and the two men in hip boots working the deck came over and looked at the shark and then each of them kicked it. The big gray body barely moved, a massive thing.

Erika wasn't here.

Winslow made his way back into town and back to the motel without seeing her. He got his nylon windbreaker from the car, the one from Kelly's Olympian, as it was starting to cool off; the afternoon rain still lingered in the air as a heavy damp, almost a haze. The smell of the Gulf. He went into the other bar—not the one he'd had dinner in—and there she was, drinking alone at the bar while a country band arranged their equipment onstage behind a chicken-wire fence.

"For the love of Pete," Winslow said. "Would you look at that."

"What?"

"Chicken wire in front of the stage," he said. "I've heard about it since I was a kid but this is the first time I've ever seen it. I thought it was mythological."

"For the love of Pete?"

"What?"

"Where does that *come* from?"

"From my grandmother Gertrude," he said. "From South Dakota or Ireland or Denmark."

"It doesn't sound Danish to me."

"What do you know?" Winslow said. He sat next to her and waved toward the bartender and then toward the bottle of Bud that Erika was holding, the universal signal, no language required. The bartender brought the beer, took the money, kept the silver and laid the paper money on the bar, all wordlessly. Winslow waved to him by way of thanks and the bartender waved back.

"Did you get anything to eat?"

"I'm fine," she said, and waved her bottle in the air.

"That's not what I asked," he said.

She looked into his eyes in the mirror behind the bar and

Winslow saw that this was as much of an answer as he was going to get.

"Did you ever figure out what we were fighting about?"

"I've known that all along," she said. "You want me to be one way and I want to be the way I am. That's all we ever fight about. The rest is just excuses."

Winslow opened his mouth to tell her she was wrong, but she wasn't wrong. He knew it. She was watching his face in the barroom mirror as he was watching hers. She was serious. She was right.

"OK," he said after a minute. "Where do we go from here?"

"We go home and start over," Erika said. "Or not. I don't know. I don't exactly have a plan."

"I don't, either."

"We never did," she said. And Winslow couldn't help noticing that they had slipped into the past tense. When? Some invisible line they had crossed without noticing. Erika was looking at his face still through the dust and haze of the back-bar mirror and she heard it, too; she made a face at him, regret mixed with a kind of gaiety. They were not all right. They were not going to be all right. But they were all right for now.

"What do you want to do?" Winslow asked her reflection.

"I want to see the band," she said. "Then we can go."

"That's fine with me," he said.

Double whiskeys, bottles of beer. They sat next to each other at the bar almost like strangers, like people who didn't have much to say to each other, each in their watery sadness. Whiskey had made him weak and cowardly, prone to sadness. Closing time.

At nine-thirty the band kicked in, a regular country-and-western band with ashtrays on the microphone stands and a pedal steel player, who was—as Winslow told Erika five or six times over the course of the night—really pretty good.

By eleven the place was packed and smoky and Winslow was going, going strong. The bartender from the oyster place was there and so was the crew from the fishing boat, still wearing their rubber hip boots, laughing and joking, dancing with their wives, or maybe somebody else's wives. The band sang about adultery and horses and drinking and Winslow sang along when he knew the words, and sometimes when he didn't. The band kicked into "I Am a Lonesome Fugitive" and Winslow felt a big wave of emotion roll over his little drunken heart: the certainty that this was the place, now was the time, knowing that this music told everything you needed to know about America. He was nearly weeping.

"The bees of the invisible!" he shouted to Erika.

"The bees of the invisible," he said again, up close to her ear, feeling the nearness of her body, her neck. "You take a feeling, you get it from the air and then you turn it into something that you can touch. Something you can read, something you can listen to. You take that feeling and you put it into the strings of a guitar."

"I believe you're drunk," she said.

"Everybody's got to believe in something," Winslow said. "I believe I'll have another beer."

"Don't go native on me, Richard. I don't think I could stand that."

Winslow was trying to think of something suitably sharp to say back to her but his brain was soft and spongy and clumped in his head like wet laundry. This was not going to work. This was not going anywhere. His thoughts buzzed around these central facts like moths to a light, returning, circling; it was impossible for Winslow to feel lightness or gaiety as Erika apparently did.

And when the band launched into something slow and sentimental, as the steel guitar began to weep and the drummer tiptoed around in brushes, Winslow felt his heart give way inside his chest and knew he could not speak. He took her by the arm and led her out onto the dance floor, crowded with the shrimpers and their wives, the deckhands still in rubber boots, the bartender from the other bar, all swaying slow and graceless to a sentimental beat. He gripped her tightly, more tightly than he wanted to, but he couldn't seem to help himself. He felt her little body against his, her head against his chest—felt how small she was and yet how tightly made and nimble, against the swaying hippopotamus of his body. Lumbering oaf, graceless fool. And yet somehow, in the center of all his hot regret, the certainty of his own foolishness, he felt a little calm place, a moment of repose. This would not go on forever but it was happening now: this music, this girl, this dance.

She said, "I wish . . ."

"What?"

"Nothing," she said, and buried her face in his chest again. They were going to end with everything unsaid, everything unfinished. We arrange things, Rilke said, and then they fall apart. We arrange them again and fall apart ourselves. They danced, and everybody danced around them, and again Winslow found that small quiet place at the heart of things, the place of peace and rest. Where we long to be, he thought, where we always and forever long to be.

The song ended and they kept drinking. They danced twice more, a fast one for Erika's amusement and then a final slow song, a moving embrace, a few scattered couples on the dance floor and a sad song about loss and cheating and not knowing what you had until you let it slip away. These country lyrics were driving their way into Winslow's brain and he found himself thinking in time with them, thinking about pickup trucks and good dogs and ex-wives and about the great big wide-open country they had crossed for no good reason. He felt expansive and American and drunk. He was holding on to a girl half his age. Everything was fine.

Halfway through the song, though, the big lights came on overhead: closing time. A collective groan came out of the crowd as their own unsightliness and drunkenness was revealed to them in the hard light.

"How did that happen?" Erika said. "I thought it was eleven o'clock."

"Time flies," Winslow said, hearing his own stupidity in his own ears, feeling drunk and blue. Why do parties have to end? But they did and they did. The long drive home, opening out before him.

Outside, they all said good night to each other, even the strangers, the deckhands and their wives. The sky had cleared completely and a warm wind was blowing up out of the south. The air now was warmer than it had been at noon, warm and soft and fragrant, a message from somewhere better.

"I'm not tired at all," Erika said.

Winslow said nothing. Although he knew himself to be exhausted, he did not wish this night to end; the air was warm and inviting, and whatever was coming next would be worse.

"What do you want to do?" he said.

"Let's go out to the beach," she said.

"I don't know," he said. "I don't know if I'm good to drive or not."

"I've seen you get home when you were way worse," she said. "Besides, all the cops are asleep."

"That's the single worst line of reasoning I have ever heard," he said.

"I'll drive if you want me to."

"No thanks," he said. "I'll drive."

They walked the sleeping streets back to the motel where the car was parked, past rusting cars and barking dogs and windows blue with the blue light of television, occasional cars on the highway at the edge of town. She hung on his arm like a handbag, some small drunk accessory, tottering along in her cowboy boots and army jacket. Winslow himself was dressed for golf in chinos and a polo shirt. He knew they looked ridiculous together, knew in fact that the casual observer would in this case be right: they did not belong together, they did not fit.

They drove out over the Gulf on a long causeway with the windows down and a pint bottle between them. Winslow didn't touch it—he was in about enough trouble already—but Erika kept it working. It was like flying, the road so long and straight, appearing magically at the edge of his headlights and then disappearing behind them into the red glow. . . . He tried the radio and got Cuba or Mexico, excitable gibberish in Spanish and then a blast of trumpet.

"We could just keep going," Erika said. "Wouldn't that be nice? It just feels crazy to think about going back up into all that snow and ice and darkness. Just keep going south."

"I think we'd run out of dry land pretty soon."

"You know what I mean."

"Besides," he said, "I think I'm supposed to be teaching next week. I think they might miss me."

"We could invite them down. The rest of the class. They wouldn't mind."

"They might."

"Besides," she said, "since when are you so responsible and earnest? They could get by without you for a week. Worse things have happened."

"And are happening still," Winslow said.

They drove out and out and at the end of the causeway they found an enormous moonlit emptiness, the sound of wind and waves and air rushing by the windows of the car. They were on an empty island, nobody home, a few yard lights in the empty houses but no cars, no movement, no sound but the wind and the small waves. A mile down the beach they came to the end of the road: a parking lot, a streetlight, a sand dune.

Winslow parked the big car—the only car in the lot—under the light, and carefully rolled his socks up and left them inside his shoes on the floor of the back seat. He noted in himself the over-careful movements of the drunk, souvenirs of a life alone. A clean car was a sign of something wrong, and his was clean all over except for the side of the front seat where Erika had sat for the last two thousand miles, littered with straw wrappers and cigarette ash. She left her boots on despite the sand and brought the pint bottle with her. They were alone on the beach, alone—as near as he could tell—for miles in any direction; and there in front of them, south, were hundreds and thousands of miles of empty horizon, a few small lights of fishing boats far out in the distance. Without touching or talking, they made their way down to the water. The low waves lapped against the shore, and the sand felt cool and soft under his feet.

"Nothing," Erika said.

"What?"

"A thousand miles of nothing," she said.

She sat down in the sand and started to tug her boots off and Winslow noted with his perpetual disapproval that she was bound to get sand in them. When would he stop? Why should he care? He was tired of his own shabby authority, his endless false self-confidence. He sat next to her, took the bottle from her and drank, and all the little stars swam around, up in the sky. King of nothing in his little robe and crown. What was that cartoon? The soft wind came up out of the Gulf and made all kinds of promises to him. The air was warm and the sand was cool.

She took the bottle back and drank and then she nested it carefully into the sand next to her, at the end of her outstretched hand. Then she took Winslow by the shoulders and pulled him down on top of her, the bulk of Winslow, the weight of his body pressing her into the sand. She kissed him then, hot and clumsy, her tongue in his mouth. Winslow felt a surge of excitement run through him that echoed in some strange and unpleasant way in his body. There was something wrong with him, he had known that all along, his own weakness and weight—but this was different, some new way to feel. He felt her body beneath him, small, *a slip of a girl* as his grandmother would say

"What was that?" he asked her, whispering.

"I felt like doing that," she said.

"There's nothing wrong with that," he said.

"Poor Richard," she said. "I shouldn't tease you."

As she said this, she reached between his legs and touched his dick where it lay half drunk and half asleep against his leg and again Winslow felt it: the surge of excitement and then the sick reverberation after, something running through his body, something unwell and weak. Little Richard came to attention under her touch but he could feel his body, uncertain, unwilling.

"I could do something for you," Erika said. "If you want me to."

"Quiet," he said.

He took her hand and gave it back to her, raised himself onto his elbows and looked down into her face. The moonlight was bright on her face and her eyes were dark and closed to him.

"You know what I want from you," he said.

"It's true."

"But I'm not going to get it."

"Get off me," she said, suddenly angry. "Get off me, Richard. You want everything your way."

"No, I don't."

They were standing then, blinking at each other in the moonlight, the small waves beating against the shore.

"We can stop," Winslow said.

"We can't seem to."

He tried to think of what to say but there was nothing. At long last they had run out of words—no words to make things better, no words to make things right. Somewhere, he thought, somewhere were the magic words that would heal the two of them, that would make her understand that he was right, that he wanted only the best for her, that he loved her. *Love*: the word came like cold water in the face, unexpected and bracing. But there it was.

Maybe that was the magic word. He doubted it.

"Look," he said. "I love you."

"I know you do," she said. "You wouldn't be doing all this crazy shit if you didn't."

She sat down in the sand ten feet away, looking out at the moonlit water. She was thinking.

After a moment she said, "I love you too."

And something hot and awful welled up in his chest, a feeling so bad and miserable that it took him a moment to recognize it as happiness. She loved him, she said so. Just saying the words out loud made it real somehow, and this certainty struck him like a blow. Until a minute ago he hadn't know this was the word for it and now here he was in love.

"You want me to give myself up, though," Erika said.

"I don't."

"You do," she said. "You have to."

Winslow came up behind her and pressed himself against her back. A line of low clouds moved across the horizon, far out in the Gulf, and the moon was doing its postcard trick of shining in a broad bright line across the water toward them. He embraced her from behind and they rested there for a moment, he could feel her relax into him, he could feel her animal warmth with his hands.

"What do we do now?" she said.

"I don't know," said Winslow; but by way of actual answer he let his hand slip up her body, let his hand cover one of her tiny breasts, the nipple clear and sharp beneath the thin fabric of her shirt.

"Don't," she said.

"I want to."

"I know what you want," she said.

He left his hand there and for a moment thought that she would let him leave it there, but she couldn't—she spun out of his embrace, taking his hand as she left him, ending next to him in the sand, still holding his hand, looking at him. She was looking at his face. She was thinking. Winslow could feel his whole future life and happiness in the balance, this one moment, this time, this now.

"I'm thinking," she said.

"I know," he said. "Stop thinking."

"Whatever you say," she said.

Without another word she dropped her jeans to the sand and—turning first to Winslow, inviting him along—walked the twenty yards of sand and out knee-deep in the black water. Bare legs shining pale in the moonlight and so thin. Too thin.

"It's warm," she said. "Feel it! Unbelievable."

Winslow sitting in the sand like a puddle of mud. What was he doing here? He had no business here, nothing to hope for. Sleeping with children.

"Come on," she said. "Richard. Please."

He could not stop himself. He could not refuse her, apparently. He rolled his chinos to his knees, knowing sadly that they would inevitably get wet, resigning himself, took a last pull off the bottle and went down to the water to meet her. Here in the country of last things.

The water was warmer than he had imagined it could be, not bathtub warm but nothing bracing or shocking about it. Erika had waded farther out as he was walking down to the water and he couldn't reach her, not without getting wet. She was standing nearly waist-deep with her back turned to him, looking out at the water, the three-quarter moon. Winslow couldn't reach her. He saw himself from the outside, fat and foolish, three in the morning and two thousand miles from anything like home. He thought of all the children asleep in their beds, all the children everywhere. All the lives he hadn't led.

But he loved her, and she loved him. She said so.

Winslow knew this might not mean anything but the word itself was something he could hold on to, something he could touch. At least he knew the name of the thing now. At least he knew what was wrong with him. And now the regret came over him again, and he knew what it was: the tens of thousands of days he had wasted before he met her, tens of thousands of days she would have to herself when he was gone. Short, short. Endless blank time before and after and he had wasted so much of what came in between. Reaching out toward her. What did he care if his pants got wet? What did he care if he failed? It didn't matter, nothing mattered, he had to try.

Winslow started toward her but he couldn't see his feet in

the dark water. He was nearly there when he stepped on something sharp, invisible in the water, a shell or broken glass, he felt it cut his instep and he gasped in quick pain. Erika heard him and turned in time to watch as he lost his balance and toppled into the water. She started to laugh—he heard her start to laugh and then he was underwater and his foot was hurt, he couldn't tell how badly, but Winslow was struck with panic. For a moment he couldn't tell which way the surface lay and he turned in the water—no more than waist-deep but he couldn't find a way out—he could feel it, the air, but he couldn't tell which way it was and then he felt her hand upon his arm and she guided him upright, dripping and gasping.

"Are you all right?" she said.

"My foot . . ."

But it wasn't his foot, though it was certainly hurt—it was something else—he couldn't tell what at first but he knew it was something else, something bad.

And then his heart exploded in his chest.

He knew at once that this was what he had come all this way for. Erika must have seen it in his face because she reached for him at once. But her face was shadowed in the moonlight and he could not see her face. This was the most important thing: to see her face, to have it in his mind. This was bad. The pain was crushing. He started back toward the sand, lunging, using her shoulder as a prop, then toppling off into the shallow water.

"Oh, shit," she said. "Oh, Richard, don't."

He opened his mouth to tell her he wouldn't but he couldn't make a sound come out.

Then Erika was pulling at him. She couldn't move him except when the small waves came shoving in to help but she was strong—she managed somehow to get him near the sand and then rolled him up into the dry sand, and then some new feeling—a giant hand, Winslow felt the giant hand around his chest and squeezing—some new spasm of pain doubled him over again and she couldn't move him. The pain was remarkable, an orgasm of pain, enveloping.

"Don't die," she said.

Again he opened his mouth to speak and again he couldn't.

"Don't do it," she said. "I love you. I'm not done with you."

He heard her through the haze of pain and immediately forgot that he was in pain at all. A surge of happiness, the greatest happiness welled up in him: she loved him, she was going to live, she was in the human circle. He had entangled her in the human circle. He had touched her. It seemed like enough—a life that had that in it was not an empty life, and not even the certainty that he would not be around to see it could interfere with the great happiness he felt. He took her hand and held it between his own hands, against his chest, and tried again to tell her that he loved her while the small waves lapped against his body, but his voice could not be made to work. He felt the smile crossing his face. He felt like a man getting married. Then he died.

In the afterlife she stays in the apartment over the garage of her stepfather's house in Menlo Park, California. There's a room for her in the house, a room with her old furniture and stuffed animals and clothes. But this is not a house she's ever lived in—her stepfather only moved here a year ago—and it's better to be a little separate, a door she can close between herself and him, twenty feet of green California grass to cross between the apartment and the house.

Besides, it's better outside. The trees were already leafed out when she moved here in April, the trees all grown up around the windows of the second-floor apartment, so it's like living in a treehouse. The sunlight moves across the floors in dappled spots and leaf shadows. A little deck sits in one corner, outside a big glass double door, and in warm weather she sits outside; in cooler weather she can sit inside and still feel the sun through the glass. She's got a kitchenette and her own bathroom and her own television, which she never uses.

What she does is once a week she has her stepfather drive her down to the Menlo Park library, as fine a library as money can buy, where she checks out a new armful of books each time. This week it's Dickens, Roethke and Poe. The plan over time is to read through all the books he mentioned, all the books he loved; she's tired of feeling ignorant, tired of nodding brightly when Winslow or anybody else would bring up some famous name and she would pretend to have read it. It's going slowly but it's going well. Dickens, for instance—who would have guessed that she would turn out to be a Dickens addict? But she burned through *Tale of Two Cities* in two days, and now is making herself read through the Roethke and the Poe before she starts in on *Hard Times*, her little reward. Though the other two are good, too. So far she's only really hated Jane Austen, the little fussbudget.

It's strange, she expects him to walk back in her door one of these days. She wants to be able to talk to him when he does. She wants to be able to keep up.

Not really. She knows he's dead. She ought to know it, after Florida. Just the word *Florida* makes her close her eyes, some combination of pain and shame and embarrassment, the touch of his body dead on the beach and she couldn't leave, couldn't go get somebody without leaving him to the waves and the water, and she couldn't do that. All night and an hour into the morning before the first dog-walker found them.

In the afterlife she sits in the sun and reads and sips mint tea and feels the lump growing inside her. They say it's a baby but she's not so sure. She wishes she could bring back Winslow for just one moment to ask him if he remembers anything of the kind. Certainly she doesn't remember—which is not to say that it didn't happen. Too many rights that tapered off into blackness. Many opportunities for mayhem.

They say the baby's all right but again she's not so sure. Actually they say that they *think the* baby is all right, that they can find nothing wrong with the baby. That's what they call it: *the baby.* Erika still thinks of it *as the lump* and thinks that in the end—as she has suspected all along—it will kill her. She is more even-minded about this prospect than she was before. She's not nearly so scared of dying, nor is she secretly attracted, *half in love with easeful Death,* as Keats would say. She love love loves Keats in the way she has always loved Dickinson. One more thing to thank Winslow for, if ever she sees him again.

In the afterlife she looks at her body in the mirror and sees a girl she doesn't recognize, soft and puffy with all the fat she's eating, the butter and whole milk and peanut butter and meat. She isn't beautiful anymore, the cow and not the knife. Fat cow. This is somehow all right, she doesn't need to be beautiful, it was never about anybody else anyway but how she looked in her own eyes, but she does miss it: the sharpness and fierceness of the way she used to look, it pleased her. But now biology is using her and she is pleased to be part of it, pleased to be used, the baby taking over the body that used to be hers. She doesn't need it anymore. The baby can have it.

Once a week her stepfather—his name is Henry—drives her into the middle part of town, where she meets with a therapist, the easily baffled Dr. Monica. Erika supposes she should be more kind toward Dr. Monica, but she lost sympathy with her right away, when she wanted to put Erika on a basket of pills with no regard for the baby.

What will the baby do if it has no mother? Dr. Monica had asked sternly, as if this never had occurred to Erika.

Erika hates stupid people and she hates people who treat her like she is stupid herself.

Henry, her stepfather, is a money guy, big house, Mercedes. He's got a girlfriend, which Erika is not supposed to know about, but who cares? Her mother has been dead three years now and besides, that was all in L.A., a long way from here. The girlfriend comes and goes at night, another reason for Erika to stick to the treehouse. The girlfriend is artistic, divorced, Erika couldn't help noticing that she had these enormous tits. Probably a sign of mental health on Henry's part; no more angry women for him but big plush American girls. She paints, the girlfriend does, and has a twelve-year-old son.

Most days Henry comes home for lunch and makes her soup and crackers. Most days he's out for dinner, either business or the girlfriend, so lunch is their main time together. It's odd; Erika never liked him much before, thought he was faceless and earnest and too much of a sucker, the way her mother used him. But now she likes him, and he seems to like her. She looks forward to their little lunches, talking about the neighborhood, whatever fresh hell was in the newspaper that morning. He's actually way over to the left of all her friends, he voted for Jesse Jackson once, it's interesting, a person with money like that. It's very quiet in the big house. One day he took her into his office and showed her the papers writing her specifically into his will and told her not to worry about money, just worry about the baby. They could work the rest of it out later.

At first Erika was suspicious. He was being nice because she looked like her mother, she reminded him of her mother. Now she believes differently. It's strange how few genuinely kind people there are in the world, and how lucky she has been to know at least two of them.

Dave came down when school ended and stayed a week.

He's coming back when the baby is born. Her best girlfriend is a boy. So what?

It's hard not drinking, though. It was hard when Dave was around, everything so hard-edged and dry and sharp. It was hard to talk. She came really close to having that one drink then, that first one. She really wanted a drink. But what she really wants is not one drink but twenty, not a little social lubrication but oblivion and death. She still likes the idea of oblivion and death but she's signed some other contract now. It's all right. She's just going to have to find some other way to live.

Crackers and soup and conversation. It's not much but it's a start. After lunch Henry goes back to work in his big blue Mercedes and Erika climbs back into the treehouse and takes a nap. It's amazing the way she can sleep now. She always hated sleep, always fought it, always needed twenty drinks to get to sleep, so she woke up wounded and sore. Now it feels like she lives to sleep, sleep sleep sleep, ten hours a night and a nap in the afternoon. It helps that Winslow comes to her in her dreams sometimes, comes and talks to her. It helps that she can remember her dreams, too.

She goes up to the treehouse after lunch and she sleeps for an hour or sometimes a little more, sleeps to the sound of the breeze in the leaves outside her window, the shifting shadows of leaves and sun across the blond wood floor. Sometimes, drifting off to sleep, she really feels that she is in the afterlife, some pleasant purgatory between the last life, which has definitely ended, and the new life that has not yet begun. It's not bad. It's not forever. She's going to have a baby. She drifts off to sleep quickly in this new life and she sleeps quietly. Her hair isn't even messed up when she awakens. The bedclothes are barely ruffled.

When she awakens she sits at the edge of the bed for a moment and tries to remember her dreams, tries to remember if he was in any of them. In dreams as in life Winslow is always telling her what to do. It still annoys her.

She gets up, makes herself another cup of hot mint tea with honey and sits at the kitchen table. Oddly enough she doesn't really miss him. She burns with regret and remorse at the time they wasted, but if they hadn't both been careless they would never have met. But she feels like he's there all the time, even when she can't see him or touch him. It's a strange feeling and she knows it doesn't make sense. One of the things she learned from him: you can only feel what you feel. It doesn't have to make sense.

What was her name? The one who would knit the world back together every evening—or did she spin? Erika can't re-member. She'll learn it eventually if she keeps up the reading. But that's what it feels like in these soft, sunny California after-noons: it feels like she's gathering the strands of the day, trying to remember what happened and why it was important, what she did and what she saw and what she felt; and, gathering the strands, she begins to work them together into a single thing, a thing made out of words, and every one of them begins the same: *Dear Richard*

A Note About the Author

KEVIN CANTY is the award-winning author of the
novels *Into the Great Wide Open* and *Nine Below Zero*, and
the short-story collections *Honeymoon and Other Stories*
and *A Stranger in This World*. His work has been
published in *The New Yorker, Esquire, GQ, Details, Story,*
the *New York Times Magazine* and *Glimmer Train*.
He lives in Missoula, Montana.

A Note About the Type

The text of this book is set in Dante, a typeface
designed by Giovanni Mardersteig in collaboration
with Charles Malin after World War II.
Mardersteig was a printer, book designer and typeface
designer, and Charles Malin is considered one of the
great punch cutters of the twentieth century.

This typeface was adapted for hot metal composition
by the Monotype Corporation in 1957. The digital
version of Dante used in this book was redrawn by
Ron Carpenter for Monotype and issued in 1993.